THE BEYOND

THE ENTANGLED SERIES
BOOK 7

JILL SANDERS

GRAYTON

This is a work of fiction. Names, characters, places, and incidents either are the product of the author's imagination or are used fictitiously, and any resemblance to actual persons, living or dead, business establishments, events or locales is entirely coincidental.

ISBN: 978-1-945100-61-1

PRINT ISBN: 9798357993892

Print ISBN: 978-1-945100-73-4

Copyeditor: Erica Ellis – inkdeepediting.com

SUMMARY

Selene never asked for the darkness that followed her all her life. It wasn't until her sixteenth birthday that something clicked, and she began to understand how to control it. She spent years jumping between foster homes, and the only steady person in her life was Scott, her foster-family brother. Finding out that she has an actual sister has been some of the only good news in her life. But when she finds out that she has a brother as well, things take a darker turn.

Scott was a lost soul. He was born into the world a bastard and would leave the world the same. But somehow he's ends up with a one-way ticket to the underworld, only he isn't dead. Yet. The only thing he regrets in his short life is not telling Selene how important she was to him.

PROLOGUE

Hell was a real place. No, really. It was. Selene knew this because she was currently standing in the Beyond, as she called it. Though she was only four and had yet to learn or hear the word *hell* yet.

One minute she'd been in the cramped bedroom that she shared with three other foster kids, and the next she was standing under a hazy red sky. The nasty purple carpet, covered in fleas and dirt, had been replaced with a brownish-black ground.

To her, this new place was an improvement. For starters, there weren't any screaming kids to pick on her. She also didn't have to hide from her foster parents when they grew angry at the noise or when one of the kids asked for food.

Here, it was quiet and, even more important, she was all alone.

In the next few years, she would return to the Beyond as often as she could. Every time she returned, life grew worse and worse for her in the real world.

Until one day. Until he came into her life.

Six-year-old Selene stood on the front porch step, her arms tucked tight against her shivering body. Her hands were shoved deep in the pockets of her worn jeans, lest anyone wanted to reach out to take her hand. She wished she still had the coat she'd worn the day before, but when she'd been kicked out of the last foster home, she'd been told to leave it and all of the other things she'd collected behind since they technically weren't hers.

The social worker knocked on the door of the trailer one more time, glancing down at Selene every so often.

"I'm sure they're home," the heavy-set woman said. She was bundled up more than Selene was and looked like a huge grape in the dark purple outfit.

If no one opened the door of the small trailer, the woman would be left to deal with Selene for the rest of the evening herself, the possibility of which she'd complained about during the entire ride from the foster care home Selene had been kicked out of.

No one wanted her. That wasn't just a lie that a little girl told herself in situations like hers. It was a fact. In the last eight months, Selene had been shuffled to eleven different foster homes.

Every time, the families explicitly told the social worker that there was something wrong with her.

Initially, Selene appeared normal, no different than the other kids she'd lived with in the old church turned foster care building. The place had smelled of urine and wet carpet, something she would never forget nor ever get over.

Even though she was only six, Selene was extremely smart. More intelligent than most of the adults whom she had been entrusted to. That in itself was the reason for more than half of the removals.

No one liked a smart girl. She'd been told that more

times than she could count. And she could count higher than there were stars in the sky.

So she'd tried to play dumb. That had only gotten her beaten and almost killed by one of her last placements. The woman was a monster. Selene had known this the moment she'd see her. But she had no say in where she was dropped off, so she'd tried to make the best of it. That placement had lasted a week. One long, grueling week.

The monster had dropped a pan of hot oil on Selene's hands. When not a single red mark appeared on her skin, the woman had called her a witch. The woman had been too afraid to explain to the agency why she no longer wanted her and how she knew that Selene couldn't be harmed.

That hadn't been the first clue that Selene was different. But it had been the first time someone had taken notice. Selene had enjoyed the fear in the woman's eyes.

The next time she was placed with a monster, she used that fear to her benefit for as long as she could. A month later, the woman and man abandoned her back at the home.

She didn't try to learn the adults' names, and when she did know them, she purposely avoided calling them by their names. It was easier that way.

Did she cause problems on purpose? Hell, yes, she did. She hated every single person that came into her life.

Why shouldn't she?

Someone had hated her enough that they had left her on the doorstep to the Nashville firehouse days after she'd been born in the first place. Her first few months of life had been at a hospital of sorts. All she could remember, and yes, she remembered most of it, was being shuffled out of a crib and into a playpen until she could sit up and crawl. No one held her. No one was there to comfort her. Her feedings were done with a pillow propping up the bottle until she learned to hold it in her hands.

She had watched in amazement and learned from the large television set hanging over her playpen. It wasn't cartoons or some other childish show; instead, she'd watched the news or the weather channel.

She'd learned to talk early, to spell shortly after that. Numbers were easy. Too easy. They'd come to her before she'd learned how to walk or run.

When the people around her found this out, she'd been tested. But she hadn't wanted to please anyone, since no one in her life had stuck around longer than a week.

No faces or voices to bond with. No warm hugs or kisses or tickles to make her giggle. There had been a serious lack of physical or emotional connection in her life.

Because of this, she had decided not to let them see what she could do. To keep it hidden. Guarded.

Much like everything else in her life.

The first time she realized what could happen to people when they touched her was the first time she was afraid. Truly afraid. Not for her own well-being, but for the lack of possibilities for her future.

She could never fall in love or have a family of her own. It had taken a year for that news to sink in. In that time, she'd acted out. Everyone had called her a spoiled child.

But she'd learned that it took too much energy to act out. She'd grown bored of the games. Of outwitting her captors. Which is what each and every one of them was to her.

They'd forced her to go to school. The last time she'd learned something new in school was when she'd stumbled across a bully that was bigger than she was. Not that she'd gotten hurt—nothing could physically harm her. But the bully had used other tactics, had gone after emotional weaknesses that Selene believed she had quashed years prior.

Selene wasn't proud of her looks. She knew what she looked like dressed in hand-me-downs with more holes in them than a wiffle ball.

Her jet-black hair had been cut to the scalp almost a year before by one of the women she'd been staying with. Now, it had grown to just past her chin. But it hadn't been trimmed and was all different lengths and stood up in places.

She was skinny. Really skinny. Like those kids she'd seen pictures of third-world countries. She didn't have kwashiorkor, which caused the swollen belly in those kids. Instead, she could see each and every one of her ribs. Sometimes she even placed a finger or two between the protruding bones.

Her face was long and square somehow. Her eyes too big, too dark. She couldn't even distinguish between the irises and the pupils when she looked in the mirror. This was another reason people did not like her. One man had claimed he could see all of his past sins in her eyes.

When he'd tried to touch her at night, he'd ended up on the floor in a fit of vomit. She was thankful when she'd been moved to another home.

Being bullied about her appearance had shamed her more than anything else could have. She wanted to be pretty more than she wanted to be smart. Why? She didn't know.

Maybe it was because everywhere she looked, people were striving to be beautiful. Maybe because it was the one thing she couldn't control. Being bullied about it caused her to cry for the first time in her life that she could remember.

The social worker banged on the door to the trailer again. "Hello? Mr. Logan."

Selene could tell the woman was getting desperate.

Just then the door was yanked open. Instead of there being an adult on the other side, it was a boy roughly her own age. He was a lot taller than her and had more muscles than she did. He was wearing white underwear and nothing else. The kid's blond hair was longer than hers and stuck out all over the place in a mess of curls.

Selene held her breath. Something deep inside her shifted. Something new formed in her soul. For the first time in her life, she felt a need to connect with someone else.

The boy looked at the social worker and then at Selene. Then he turned and yelled, "Dad! We got another one."

CHAPTER ONE

T*en years later...*
There was no way she was going back. Selene knew her worth. Knew that she was smarter than anyone else at the party. For good measure, she threw up her middle finger as a ton of drunk kids watched her from the bonfire.

This was the last time she'd allow Scott to convince her to tag along with him, she told herself as she stomped away. She didn't need friends. Didn't need anyone else to solidify her worth on this stupid planet.

She kept telling herself that as she marched past the row of cars. She needed movement. Needed speed.

She was so preoccupied with her anger that she forgot to make sure the coast was clear before taking off into the night sky. The cool wind on her face, tangling her long jet-black hair, took that anger down a notch. Closing her eyes, she went beyond the layer of clouds that hovered just above the lake where the group of friends, none of them hers, had partied each weekend for the past few months.

Tonight, she'd been a tagalong. Thanks, Scott. She was his plus one. She was the poster child for girls that need help making friends. Well, this was the last time she'd allow him to talk her into anything.

The moment she had stepped foot in the ring of firelight earlier, she knew she'd made a mistake.

Scott had let Cristy pull him into the darkness near the water's edge while his "friends" had done their worst. These weren't her people. Would never be. She should have never dreamed she could fit in. Anywhere.

Almost half an hour later, she softly touched down, her toes landing in the exact same spot she'd pushed off from. Her heart still ached from the rejection, but her emotions were finally back under control.

"What in the hell, Selene," someone said behind her. She jerked around.

Scott stood exactly where she'd left from half an hour earlier, his arms crossed over his chest and a look on his face that told her she was in deep trouble.

She wasn't concerned that he'd seen her fly. After all, he'd been there when she'd discovered that particular power. He'd also been there when she'd discovered all the other odd things about herself. He knew everything about her. Every odd little detail of who she was.

"It's almost your birthday, and I thought you'd want to hang. Instead, you take off." He motioned to the sky.

She wanted to point out the humor because he was upset that she had taken off and not concerned that someone could have seen her flying.

"You took off first with Cristy," she pointed out.

"She just pulled me aside to give me..." He frowned. "Never mind." He shook his head and took Selene's hand to pull her towards the party again.

"Nope." She jerked her hand free.

She never let anyone touch her, though usually Scott

was the exception. It just usually didn't end well. It was just one of the odd things about her, in addition to the flying. And flying wasn't her only power. She just hadn't figured out how to control the others like she could control flight. Yet. There was also the fact that she was the goddess of darkness. Or so her real parents always said when they mystically and magically visited her.

"I am not going back there." She crossed her arms over her chest. "They're a bunch of idiots."

"Selena, it's..."—he looked at his phone—"five minutes until your birthday." He moved closer to her.

From the first moment she'd seen him, he'd had a way of calming her down. As far as anyone knew, they were brother and sister. No matter what had happened, they had stuck together, even through all the foster homes they had bounced around in over the past ten years. And there had been plenty.

One short year after she'd arrived at his doorstep, his adopted foster father, the kindest soul she'd ever met, had died of a heart attack, leaving Scott and her in a mess.

For over a month, they'd avoided the knocks on the trailer's door. They'd lived how they wanted to, free of any adults. But after they ate every bit of food in the trailer then, they got hungry.

At first, the agency had talked of separating them. But then Scott did something that had surprised her. He'd held onto her and yelled that they would just run away if they weren't kept with one another. So they'd been shuffled from home to home, together.

"I just wanted to do something nice for you. It's your sixteenth birthday," he said as if she didn't already know.

"So? I've never had a birthday celebration before. I don't

need to start now." But somewhere deep down, her heart ached for just that.

Cristy had hosted a massive party last month for her sweet sixteenth. Everyone in the school had been invited. Well, almost everyone.

Still, she'd heard all about the wonderful party from Scott. He'd tried to convince her to go with him then too. Thankfully, she hadn't.

"Here," Scott said, holding out a small package. "This is what I was talking to Cristy about."

Selene looked down at the small bundle in his hands. It was no bigger than a baby bird and she in no way wanted to take it from him. But he shoved the wrapped gift in her hands.

"I... well, I bought it," he finished, avoiding her eyes.

"From Cristy?" Selene wanted to toss it to the ground. To step on it until whatever was inside was in a million pieces.

Scott might be fooled by Cristy's pretty blonde hair, perfect cheerleader body, and sweet southern-belle voice. Selene was not.

"No." He shook his head. "I had her buy it for me. Since... Well, are you going to open it or aren't you?"

She took a deep breath. This was the very first present anyone had gotten her. Ever.

She peeled off the plain silver wrapping paper and tossed it to the ground. She wanted to keep it. Fold it up and lock it away with her other small keepsakes. But she didn't want Scott to know that.

Inside was a small black box held closed by a black piece of material.

"It's a hair tie. A scrunchie. Your hair is getting longer

and, well, I thought you'd like it," he said. "Open the box now."

She looked at the small rubber band covered by material and felt her eyes sting. She hadn't been able to afford anything fancy for her long hair, so she'd always just used rubber bands that she'd found on the ground. They'd get tangled in her hair and, on several occasions, Scott had had to cut them out of her long tresses. Selene put the scrunchie on her wrist and opened the box.

Her heart skipped and then burst. Inside was a bottle of purple nail polish. She looked up at Scott.

"I know it's your favorite color." He looked down at the bottle as a tear streamed down her cheek. "Don't get weird about it. It's just... well..." He shifted, looking very uncomfortable. "Happy birthday." He suddenly walked over and wrapped his arms around her.

They had hugged a few times in their lives, to comfort one another during a bad time or to celebrate getting into a good home together. This hug was nothing like those in the past. This one was... softer somehow.

For the past few years, she'd felt a drive to him that hadn't been there earlier. She'd chalked it up to puberty and the fact that everyone else their age was making out all the time and talking about sex. Hell, she knew Scott had been making out with girls for years now.

She'd tried to hide her jealousy. Tried. But it stung. Part of her knew that she would never, could never, have that bit of normalcy. To be touched. To touch. To kiss. Maybe that's what was at the core of her thoughts about Scott. Maybe it was just because he had something she never could.

The longer she told herself that, the more miserable she grew.

But then Scott totally shocked her by pulling away

slightly and, after locking eyes with her, gently laying his lips over hers. She knew it wasn't meant as anything other than a brotherly kiss, but the moment their lips touched, something strange happened.

It was as if the simple touch supercharged her. She could feel energy pulsing from Scott's lips through her own, spreading down to her core. And for the first time in her life, everything went white. One minute she was standing by the lake next to Scott, holding her birthday gifts, and the next she was standing on a grassy hillside.

She blinked a few times to make sure she wasn't hallucinating. Then she saw the girl. She was roughly Selene's age. But instead of worn jeans, a ratty T-shirt and sweatshirt, and shoes with holes in them, this girl was wearing a dress. A fancy dress. The kind that Selene had seen and drooled over in the teen magazines at the bookstores.

"Hello?" Selene called out to the girl, but it was as if no sound had come out. The girl blinked a few times, then cried out as if in pain as she turned in circles. She threw her arms up in the air as if she was afraid the full moon overhead was going to attack her. Then she sank down into the soft grass and cried.

For the second time in her life, Selene wanted to help someone else. She took a step towards the girl, but just as quickly as she had gone away, she was back in Scott's arms, his lips still on hers.

"What the..." She jerked away from him and stumbled backwards. Not because of the kiss. Never because of the kiss. But looking into Scott's eyes, she could tell that's exactly what he thought was wrong.

How could she tell him what had just happened to her? One more weird thing about her. Great.

"I..." She glanced around and realized she'd dropped

the box with the nail polish in it. She bent down and scooped it up, along with the wrapping paper, and without saying a word to Scott, she shot up into the dark night sky.

"Happy birthday, Selene," she heard Scott call after her.

Ten years later...

Selene sat in the stuffy office and waited with everyone else. There were three businessmen in dark suits, all wearing shoes that had no doubt been shined just for the day, and shirts and ties that had been pressed just for this occasion. The two businesswomen in the room looked even more nervous than the men.

Maybe it was because they knew that whatever job they were interviewing for, they'd get ten percent less pay than any of the men in the room. It was the south. That's just the way it was around here.

She looked down at her leather pants, black boots, and leather jacket and smiled. Hell yes, she stuck out like a sore thumb.

She wasn't here today to apply for some stuffy job. She was here because she had to go somewhere and do something, and she'd made a stupid promise a long time ago.

When the secretary stepped out to call the next name, she stood up. It had been almost five minutes since anyone had come out the locked door, and she was not going to wait another five minutes.

"I need to see Scott Logan," she said firmly.

The woman ran her eyes over Selene's outfit quickly before blocking the door and asking, "Name?"

"Selene, I'm his sister," she said firmly. "It's a family emergency." Okay, so she'd gotten really good at lying. It wasn't as if uptight secretary in heels even cared. No, she'd already put Selene in her who-cares-who-the-fuck-you-are category.

Without waiting for a response, Selene pushed past her and rushed down the hallway towards Scott's corner office.

When she stepped in, he was sitting on the edge of the desk, his face away from the doorway. There was a very busty brunette woman standing between his thighs. The woman had her hands on his shoulders as if she was leaning in for a kiss.

Selene cleared her throat, and the woman glanced over at her as Scott jumped up from the desk.

"Sorry to interrupt," Selene said sarcastically.

During all those years that Selene had been the outcast, Scott hadn't been. He'd been the most popular kid in every single grade and sport he'd been in. He'd excelled at every-thing. Which had been his big ticket out of the hellhole life they had called home. He'd gone to college in Atlanta and had gotten a high-paying job immediately after, where he, of course, had climbed to a top position.

"Selene," Scott gasped as she leaned against the door frame.

Damn, he looked good. He was wearing a suit like all those stiffs out in the lobby were. Only his screamed he had money. More than they had ever had. More than she had.

His blond hair had darkened some and was longer on the top than he used to wear it, which allowed the curls she'd always loved to show. His blue eyes searched hers and that sexy little dimple in his cheek flashed for just a moment before it was gone. As if he remembered he was supposed to be mad at her.

The brunette appeared very agitated at the disturbance.

Especially now that it appeared that Scott was no longer interested in her.

"Fun times in the office?" Selene asked.

"Thanks, Stacie." Scott turned to the woman. "I'll let you know later this week."

Stacie eyed Selene up and down. Selene had seen the look so many times from women before that it no longer fazed her. "Yeah, thanks, Stacie," Selene said, lacing her words with sarcasm.

When the woman stepped past her, Selene smiled brightly, then shut the door in the woman's face.

"What the hell is wrong with you?" Scott asked as he sat down behind his desk. "And what are you doing in Atlanta? Last I heard you were in... Tennessee." His eyes narrowed.

Damn. The guy just kept getting better with age. She'd gone an entire year without seeing him and—boom!—all those old feelings flooded back at her the second she saw him again. How the fuck was she supposed to be normal around the guy?

"You're not even listening to me," Scott said, rolling his eyes.

"I'm only here because I'm a woman who keeps my promises," she said, not caring what he'd been saying earlier. She'd made a promise and, by the gods, she was going to keep her promise, even though she hated being here, hated seeing him again.

Scott stilled and a frown caused those sexy lips that had once kissed her to dip downwards. "You're doing something? Going somewhere?"

"Yup." She nodded and sat on the edge of his desk. "So, I'm here to let you know."

His eyes narrowed and his sexy Adam's apple bobbled

as he swallowed. Everything about him was sexy. Too sexy. Too damned sexy.

"Tell me," he said, and she knew that she wouldn't get away without at least giving him the basics.

"You know the blonde girl I saw on my sweet sixteenth?" she started. It had taken her almost a year to tell him the story of what had happened to her during that kiss. Her first kiss. She couldn't keep anything from him.

"Yes," he answered slowly.

"She... reached out to me. I finally know where she is. I had a... calling," she said casually, as if she'd just received an invite from a close friend via text message or a phone call instead of a ring of power made of light that shot at her like a beacon when she'd been fast asleep.

"Calling?"

"A pulse wave. Sort of." She shrugged. "Call it what you want. She's in a town called Hidden Creek." She didn't want to go into the details of how she knew the name of the town. Even she didn't know how she knew.

"I know of it," he said, starting to get up.

She placed her hands on his shoulders, right where Stacie's had been seconds ago. "Nope," she said, nudging him back into his seat. "You're staying put. This is mine," she said, meaning it.

"Selene," he warned, but she stopped him by shaking her head. "I don't know anything more. I could be walking into a trap." She leaned closer and lowered her voice. "And I'm the only one of us that is indestructible. Remember?"

Scott sighed and closed his eyes for a moment. When he opened them, they were focused on hers. "Be careful. The moment you feel like something has gone south, I can be there."

She smiled and stood up straight, prepared to leave. But he stopped her by taking her hand.

"It's good to see you," he said softly, throwing her off balance.

"Yeah." She focused on his fingers touching her skin. It still shocked her when he touched her. It always would. She looked into his eyes and relaxed.

"You were expecting…"—he dropped off and looked at their joined fingers—"things to change in that area?"

"Yeah." She sighed, and he smiled. Damn him. Why did he have to be so fucking sexy?

"Will you come back here?" he asked suddenly.

"Nope." She shook her head. "This is a one-time visit. I kept my promise. I told you." She pulled her hand from his gently. She wanted to tell him that seeing him here, like this, with Stacey or any other woman drooling over him, stung too much. Instead, she bit her lip and let her heart sink further into her chest. Hidden away forever.

"Thank you," Scott said softly.

She turned and, without another word, left him one more time.

The last time she'd done so, it had broken something deep inside her. This time, whatever had remained intact shattered the moment she shut the door behind her.

CHAPTER TWO

Scott cursed himself for not going after Selene. It had been two days since she'd left his office, and he'd only received a handful of text messages from her.

"The blonde girl is my sister."

He'd called her, but she'd ignored him. So, he'd replied back.

"Answer, damn it."

"Can't," came her response the next morning. "We're having a fun family reunion. Saving the universe and all that. Gotta go."

When had they grown apart? From the moment she'd shown up at the door to the trailer, the two of them had been inseparable.

His adopted father had been a kindhearted man, had opened his doors to kids who couldn't be placed into a foster care home. Basically, all the rejects.

And after a few weeks with Selene, he'd known just why she'd been titled as such. She was different. Really different.

The first time he noticed was when she picked up a

boiling pan and set it on the countertop without so much as a red mark on her. The second time was when a teacher grabbed Selene's wrist to discipline her for mouthing off, even if it was just because Selene had corrected the woman's math. The teacher's eyes had turned a milky white. Then she'd dropped her hold on Selene and had backed into a corner, screaming so loudly that the principal had rushed into the class.

From then on, no one touched Selene. No one except him. They held hands, they played together, they helped one another.

When he went to wake his foster father one morning and found him lying on the floor, Scott knew they were screwed. So, he'd done what he thought had been best for him and Selene. He'd locked the door and stuffed towels under it.

He knew what happened to kids like them. He'd lived with other foster families until he'd been six. He couldn't remember much, but he remembered how terrible it was.

He didn't know the reason he'd been left alone in the world, but he'd been shipped from foster home to foster home until finally ending up on Mark Logan's doorstep.

If he and Selene were found living there alone, they'd get separated and shipped off again. Something deep down told him that he had to stay with Selene.

They'd tried to keep their foster father's death a secret. It had worked for a little over a month. They'd gotten themselves to the school bus on time, packed their lunches, did laundry and dishes, and even cleaned the trailer better than when the old man was alive.

Then the social worker started banging on the door. They'd hidden and remained quiet the first few times. But then the power and water had been shut off. They had been too young to realize that bills still had to be paid.

In the end, they had run out of food and out of time together. They had been shuffled into a large building that Selene told him she'd been at many times before. It smelled worse than the trailer had when they'd left.

Thankfully, they were still together, and he'd figured the place wasn't as bad as Selene had made it out to be. They had food. Water. School. Friends.

For several months, he'd enjoyed it. Until one day, he had been told to collect his things. He was going to be placed at a home.

He went and packed up his backpack and then went and found Selene, excited that they were going to be together. But she hadn't packed. She hadn't been told she was going.

Something deep inside him clicked. He started screaming. Started fighting until the family agreed to take Selene too.

It wasn't long after their third placement that Selene woke him one night claiming there was a large snake man in her bedroom. She'd crawled in bed with him, and he'd held her shivering body until they'd both fallen fast asleep.

The next day, she'd told him about the man called Typhon, who claimed to be her father.

"He told me that I'm the goddess of darkness. I don't want to be a goddess." She'd pouted.

After that day, other things changed about Selene. For one, he caught her levitating over her bed one day. She was just sitting there reading and hadn't even known she was doing it.

Then, one night, the power had gone out in the apartment they were living in. The foster parents had rushed in with a flashlight and taken them to the living room to wait out the storm together. But when they went in to get Selene, it was as if the light from the flashlight wouldn't penetrate through the darkness surrounding her.

The next morning, the foster parents returned them to the home.

Shortly after his fifteenth birthday, they finally found the home they would remain in until they both graduated from high school. The Lindseys were an older couple and pretty much let them do whatever they wanted.

They lived in an old farmhouse on the outskirts of town. Scott immediately joined every sport he could and became popular, while Selene grew more distant and reclusive.

He did what normal teenage boys did—acted out as much as he could. He flirted and slept with any girl who gave him attention. Meanwhile, Selene hid her secrets from the world and had the weight of the secret of her abilities on her shoulders.

He knew how she must feel, being unable to touch anyone. What those abilities made her feel, how alone in the world she must have felt. Then the night of her sixteenth birthday changed the way he looked at her.

He'd gone out of his way to get her the nail polish and the scrunchie. Well, he'd asked Cristy to do it so no one would see him buying girlie products.

Cristy had only done it because the gifts were for his sister. He knew no one liked Selene. He also understood that Selene didn't want to try to be friends with anyone. She had separated herself for a reason.

"It's easier this way," she'd told him when he'd invited her to another party. "If someone happens to touch me or I screw up and show anyone what I can do, we'll have to move again."

He couldn't argue with that. The only reason they had stayed so long with the Lindseys was because Selene had distanced herself from everyone.

She was incredibly smart—like, super genius—but she hid that ability from their teachers. She got just enough answers wrong on her tests to stay under the radar.

Every single time his grades slipped, Selene would step in and help him get through his classes so that he could do well enough to remain in sports.

It was because of sports that he'd gotten the scholarships to college. He had wised up a lot that first year living in the dorms. No more goofing off for him.

Selene had left the Lindseys as well. She'd taken a job at a motorcycle shop. When that didn't pan out, she'd become a bartender at a dive bar.

Over the next few years, they saw each other a few times. She bounced around from job to job, while he continued to climb the ladder at the firm he'd been hired at.

Then, one night over a year ago, she'd showed up on his doorstep.

She'd rung the doorbell frantically, waking him up. He'd opened the door in nothing but his boxer briefs, much like the first time he'd met her.

It was storming out so badly, it had taken him a moment to realize it was Selene standing on his doorstep.

"Did you see it?" she asked, her long dark hair soaked from the evening rain. She was wearing all black. Not that that was anything new for her. She had always worn dark colors. Now she was in tight black jeans, a band T-shirt, and a leather jacket. She looked damn good.

"What?" he asked, blinking the sleep from his eyes.

"The moon." She motioned to the dark sky.

He glanced up at the dark cloudy sky and shrugged.

"Nice to see you too." He motioned for her to come in out of the rain.

"Did you see it?" she asked again, stepping past him.

"No, it's cloudy. How am I supposed to see the moon?" He pulled on a pair of his jeans.

"You live like a slob," she said, kicking a pair of his shoes by the door.

"It's a one-room studio. What do you expect?" he said with a yawn. "Coffee?"

She nodded. "You didn't see it then?"

"No," he said, and she looked deflated as she sat down on his sofa.

"How long are you going to be in town?" he asked her as he pulled out two coffee mugs. She didn't answer him, so he turned around to look at her. "I've seen you twice in the past year," he pointed out. "Where are you living now?" He handed her a cup of coffee and walked back to make one for himself.

"Tennessee," she answered quickly. Since he was turned away from her, he couldn't tell if she was lying or not. She had a tell, he knew. A small glimmer in her dark eyes that he alone could see.

Taking his cup of coffee, he moved over and sat next to her. She was correct—his place was a mess. He'd been so busy working on his last project, he hadn't taken any time to clean up. He'd had no personal life in the last few months, so he hadn't any reason to clean the place. No women in his life to worry about impressing.

He felt embarrassed that Selene was seeing the place the way it was now.

"What are you doing in Tennessee?" he asked.

"Working," she said, avoiding his eyes.

"Selene." He waited until she looked up at him. "Why are you here?"

She set the mug down and then looked down at her fingers. When she was scared, she fidgeted like she was doing now. Setting his own mug down, he took her hands. She tensed. She always had when he touched her. Then, when he didn't scream or freak out, and his eyes didn't turn a milky white, he felt her relax.

"You're worried. What did you see tonight about the moon?" he asked. Over the years, he'd learned to roll with the weirdness that came with her.

She took a deep breath. "The end is coming, Scott. It's closer than it's ever been." Her eyes met his and he could see she was telling the truth. "My parents..."

"Typhon, the father of monsters, and Rhea, the mother of gods." He'd done his homework after she'd told him about her first run-in with the deities. He still wasn't sure he believed her that they were her parents. Sure, she had superpowers, but gods as parents? For some reason, his mind just couldn't wrap around that part.

"Yes," she sighed and leaned back on his sofa.

"And... you just happened to be in Atlanta tonight to see whatever you saw the moon do?" he asked.

She glanced at him. "I flew here."

He tensed. "We talked about this," he warned.

"I know." She sat up again. "I was careful. I swear."

"Selene, one grainy picture of a woman outside an airplane is all it takes." He remembered the time she'd almost hit a jetliner. After that, they'd agreed that flying would be limited to short-distance emergency trips and only after confirming no one was looking.

"I know." She walked over to look out his window.

Then she jerked back around to him. "The moon was falling."

He frowned. "Falling?"

She wrapped her arms around herself and looked more scared than he'd seen her before. "Yes, it was... massive. It was heading directly towards me. I... felt its power growing in me. It was..." Her eyes closed.

He walked over to her and held onto her. They hadn't left on best of terms last time. She'd been angry at him for one stupid thing or another. Probably something he'd done. He was always pushing her away. Pissing her off.

It was a self-defense move he had when it came to her. If he didn't push her away, he'd try to kiss her again and, after that night on her sixteenth birthday, he couldn't chance it. Not if it meant being rejected by her again. Not if it meant losing her.

"Scott, it's all going to end soon. Everything. Not just this world, but any other out there," she said against his chest.

"Do you really think there are other worlds?" he asked.

She leaned back and looked into his eyes. "Yes."

Her deep hazel eyes drew him in. They always had. Everything he'd felt for her wanted to burst out of his chest every time she looked at him. Instead, he dropped his hands to his side and took a step back. "Selene, you'd better stay here for the night. At least until it stops raining."

He'd been an idiot back then, and he'd been one a few days ago when he'd let her walk out of his office and his life once more.

He had done a lot of research on the town she'd mentioned, Hidden Creek. It was less than a hundred miles from Atlanta. In the middle of nowhere. Yet, somehow, the small town had been all over the news in the past few years.

Everything from cults, murders, to the suspected super-natural.

Which made his worry for Selene triple.

Selene wasn't responding to his texts, so he was going to tie up some loose ends at work and head down there himself. He'd worked a double shift trying to close out his latest accounts.

He had just let himself into his studio apartment when he felt his entire body tingle.

Then, before he could react or respond, he was somewhere else.

Instead of being just inside his apartment door, he stood in a silo, the kind he'd seen on a few old movies. Only this one didn't have a massive missile inside. There was a group of strangers standing around him in a circle, all looking at him as if it was the most natural thing in the world that he'd just... appeared out of thin air. There was another man in the middle of the circle, looking just as confused and slightly pissed as well.

Then he glanced upward and saw Selene and a blonde woman floating high above them, unconscious.

"What the hell?" he asked, just before everything went black.

CHAPTER THREE

S elene stood in the darkness and listened to the blonde woman she'd seen on her sixteenth birthday talk to a man. She'd decided to leave her car in town and fly to where she could feel the pulse of power that the woman was emitting. It was stronger now, the feel of it changing the closer she got.

When she'd arrived in Hidden Creek, it was as if a piece of her that had been missing had slipped into place. There was obviously something about the town that went deep. She itched to slip into the Beyond and see what was causing so much power, but first, she had to find out what was going on and who the blonde woman was.

She would explore those avenues later. For now, she shot up into the night hair and closed her eyes, allowing the pulse to lead her to where she needed to be.

Seeing a group of people standing around in an open muddy field, she landed quietly several yards away and listened to them argue about meeting in a silo the following night.

Closing her eyes, Selene felt her heart stop. For the past

year, she'd seen this field. Had visions of the silo. She'd witnessed what was about to happen in her nightmares. This was the place. These were the people. Tomorrow night, everything would end.

When she opened her eyes again, she saw a soft green light radiating from Tara, the blonde woman she'd been seeing most of her life. The light surrounded the group and they all stood still, as if it was a perfectly normal thing. No one freaked out. No one shouted or ran. When it was gone, a large man named Joe joked about using the power to buy a house.

Everyone chuckled. What the hell? How did these people not freak out when power was displayed? Selene wanted to know more. She took a step closer just as the other four people left in a flash. The big man and the woman that he was with zipped away, heading back towards the town.

If she didn't have powers herself, she wouldn't have been able to see them because of the speed at which they were moving. But she could see a dim orange light follow them, leaving a trail behind.

The other couple shimmered for a second before disappearing. A dull green light folded around them before they disappeared.

Finally, only Tara and the man she was with stood alone in the field.

"Why did you lie to them?" the guy asked Tara. "They made a pact not to help, so why tell them to meet at the silo?"

"It's for their own good," Tara answered. "All of them. Even though they made the pact, something tells me they will try to reach us, and I just can't take that chance. I won't let them. It's too important."

Selene took another step forward. At that moment, she felt her power being connected with Tara's. She knew in that instant that the other woman knew she was there. She could no longer hide or run away. Something told her that Tara would hunt her down now that they had connected. There was no undoing what had been done. As if by that connection, Selene instantly knew that they were sisters, knew without a doubt that they came from the same place.

"We won't be alone," Tara said, turning to Selene. Even though she was shrouded in darkness, her sister's eyes locked with her own. "Hello, Selene. Sister, why don't you come forward?"

The man pointed his flashlight towards her. With a wave of her fingers, the light snuffed out.

"Light won't penetrate darkness," she said, stepping forward. "And I am the goddess of darkness." She ran her eyes over her sister, the woman she'd been seeing for twenty years. The one she'd witnessed crying in the field the first time Scott had kissed her. "You're Tara," she said, stopping a foot from them. "I've seen you," she admitted.

"You have?" Tara asked. A look of surprise flashed in her eyes. "This is my first time seeing you," Tara said. Then she shocked Selene by walking over and wrapping her arms around her. "I've always wanted a sister," Tara said softly.

Selene glanced over at the man, a little taken aback. The guy just shrugged and smiled at her as if it was normal behavior.

"I'm Colt," he said, holding out his hand when Tara released her and stepped back.

Selene glanced down at his hand. "Trust me, you do not want me to touch you."

"Okay," he said easily, dropping his hand. Her dark eyes

narrowed slightly at that. "When did you get into town?" he asked her.

"A few minutes before your friends left. Nice tricks, by the way," Selene said. "Speedster and..."

"Teleportation," Tara answered.

"You?" Colt asked.

Selene's eyes moved to him again. "Something like that. I guess the party is tomorrow, huh?" Selene sighed, knowing full well what was coming.

"Yeah." Tara nodded. "What do you know?"

Selene glanced around, suddenly feeling tired. She'd driven straight through after leaving Scott's office. Plus, the cooler night air made her realize she was tired and hungry. "Got any place a little... warmer we can talk?"

"We've got a hotel room. Where are you staying?" Colt asked.

"A hotel is good. I'll see about getting a room for myself," Selene answered.

"Do you have a car?" Colt asked as they started walking back through the field towards his truck.

"It's back in town," Selene answered.

"How did you get here then?" Tara asked. "Not that it's out of the norm. You did see our other friends. But I'm curious," Tara said as they all climbed into the truck.

"I flew," Selene said easily. Something told her that Tara had a few tricks up her sleeve as well. After all, she had shot a ring of light out earlier.

"I can fly too," Tara said eagerly.

"You can?" Selene asked, curious. "What else?"

"I'm strong. Like, really strong," Tara said.

"Check." Selene nodded.

"I can sort of shoot light..." Tara held up her hand and created a small ball of light.

"Nope." Selene shook her head. "Cool, but... She reached over and snuffed out the light. "I'm more into darkness. I sort of fold it around light."

"Okay, that's cool," Tara said with a slight frown as they parked in front of the hotel.

"I can't get hurt. I've never been sick a day in my life," Selene admitted after getting out of the truck.

Tara was silent. "Seriously?"

"I'm... going to go check in," she said, feeling stupid suddenly. She'd never told anyone about her powers. Except Scott. Even he didn't know everything that she could do. She'd fooled herself into believing she was protecting him in some way. But she knew it was only to protect herself.

After she had gotten a hotel room, she followed her sister into their room.

They were so different in appearance, but deep down, Selene knew that they were connected. Just as she'd known the moment that she'd looked at Scott all those years ago.

Tara was your typical California goddess with her blonde hair, tan skin, and blue eyes. She appeared very comfortable around people, as if she had no issues with fitting in. Unlike Selene.

They talked briefly about a few things—their parents, what visions she'd had about what was going to happen—then Tara hit her with a shocking revelation.

"You mentioned back in the field that you're the goddess of darkness. Why?" Tara asked her.

Selene glanced down at her hands remembering what the father of monsters, her father, had said to her in one vision back when she'd been ten.

"You, my daughter, are made with the darkest of dark material I could find. I traveled to the Beyond and gathered as much of it as I could to form you." The giant serpent man had smiled at her, showing fangs as long as her legs. "No light shall ever reach or penetrate you."

Selene shook the memory from her mind and looked at Tara.

"It's what Typhon has called me from the beginning. Another gift of mine is that I can't be seen in the dark. No matter how bright the light, it won't penetrate the darkness that surrounds me."

"Where I come from, Selene and Tara were twin moons," Tara said, and Selene frowned at her words. "They were beacons in the night sky, watching out for and protecting all below."

"Where you come from?" Selene shook her head, not understanding.

"I'm from another world. I think Mason called it a parallel universe. That's the best way to describe it. Another planet, similar in almost every way to this one. Rhea hid me there, or so she claims, with a man I believed was my father. I had a normal life until my sixteenth birthday, when I appeared here. In this world."

"In your ruined prom dress," Selene added, understanding so much more now. Then she remembered the other people Tara had met with in the field. Did they all have powers too? "Your friends," Selene asked after a moment, "are like us?"

"In a way," Tara answered.

Selene's eyes moved to Colt, even more curious. "And you?"

"Nope, normal boring human with no extra powers," he answered with a smile.

"That's not strictly true," Tara said. "We're fated. We've been together all throughout history." She took up his hand.

"Like reincarnation?" Selene asked, thinking about how she'd felt around Scott. How she'd known from the first moment she'd seen him that he was hers. That they were meant to be in some way.

"Something like that," Tara replied. "Whatever it is, we're meant to do this together."

"And the others?" Selene asked.

"Yes, but it's complicated. Some of them have families. We don't want to jeopardize that."

Selene was quiet for a moment. She'd remembered seeing others of power in the mist before. Not in real life, but she'd felt them. Another gift of hers was that she could hunt them out in her mind. At least the ones that were using their powers when she looked. "I've seen them before. I've spent a lifetime looking..."—she shook her head—"for a sliver of normalcy. For anyone who might understand what I was going through."

"You don't have to be alone anymore," Tara assured Selene. "I'm here."

She hated feeling vulnerable. Hated that her emotions were so raw. She needed time to get herself under control.

"Thanks." Selene avoided their eyes. "I left in such a hurry when I got your call. I drove straight here."

"My call?" Tara asked.

"A burst of power that showed me exactly where you were. A few days ago," Selene answered.

"Where did you come from, exactly? How far away from Hidden Creek?" Tara asked.

Selene shrugged. "Atlanta. I was... visiting a friend." She had been in Atlanta, but the real truth of it seemed too dark. She'd headed there to see Scott one last time before the end of everything. She hadn't wanted it all to end without at least telling him how she'd felt about him, but then she'd walked in on Scott and the blonde. Selene needed time to think. Time to rest before what was coming. Reaching for the door, she said, "Goodnight."

Instead of going back to her room, she stepped behind the hotel and flew off to get her car.

She stopped at the small grocery store that was still open and grabbed some basics. She was starved, so it was mainly junk food.

When she finally climbed into bed later, she shot Scott a text message. There was so much she wanted to tell him, but the last year being away from him made her realize that she should keep her conversations brief. After all, he had a normal life and deserved to be happy up until the very end.

"The blonde girl is my sister." She read it several times before finally hitting send.

Then she shut down for the night.

The next morning, she sat in a diner with Tara, Cole, and a bunch of other people she didn't know. Some of them she recognized from the field the night before.

The fact that no one was looking at her strangely was a plus.

At first, they asked her questions about where she'd come from and her life. She kept her answers vague. But then Jessica walked over and flipped off the open sign on the shop. The moment the group was alone, the questions changed.

"We don't mean to pry, but every new member has to go through a little trust test," the shop owner, Jess, said.

Then Xtina, a raven-haired woman, held out her hands towards Selene. "Do you mind?"

Selene's looked at her in question then warned, "Things don't go well when people touch me."

"Yeah, I forgot to ask you about that last night," Colt said. "Tara didn't seem to be affected."

Selene looked down at her hands. "I guess she's an exception."

"What happens?" Jess asked.

"The best I can tell is that people see their worst nightmares when they touch me," Selene answered. "Sort of a glimpse into their own madness."

She remembered the first time it had happened to someone. She'd been four. One of the foster moms had wanted her to sit on her lap while they watched cartoons. The woman had screamed and thrown her to the ground. The next week she'd been placed into a different home.

From then on, any time someone got close to her, they screamed in fear and usually ran away in one form or another.

"I'll chance it," Xtina said. "Just as long as you don't mind my gift of seeing your memories."

Selene was interested in this. Could the woman really see someone's past by just touching them? If so, then this was the first time she'd met anyone with abilities close to her own. "Everyone?"

"Everyone except my husband." Xtina smiled and motioned towards her husband, Mike.

Selene was quiet for a moment as she thought about Scott. For as long as she'd known him, he'd never been affected. "There is one person I've never affected besides Tara," she said quietly. Then she reached out and laid her hand in Xtina's.

Something strange happened the moment she touched hands with the woman. For starters, Xtina didn't jerk away with fear. Then, images flashed through Selene's mind like a movie on fast-forward.

By the time Xtina leaned back and broke their connection, Selene knew that the woman had seen most of her childhood and life. She'd never felt so raw and exposed around anyone before. Except Scott.

"We can trust her," Xtina said, looking deep in her eyes, and Selene knew without a doubt that she could trust everyone in the room in return.

At eight thirty that evening, Selene stood in the middle of the field with the rest of the gang.

"Put me where you want me," Selene had said to the group. "No matter what happens, tonight we'll all be fighting for our lives."

In the end, the players had been moved around like pawns. Selene and Tara were the major pieces.

"Why here?" Selene asked when they stopped walking in the field.

"It's where we were conceived," Tara answered, motioning around them.

It was? Here? Why here? So many questions ran through her mind, but she knew time was running short. Glancing up into the night sky, she added, "My power is stronger at the full moon." She turned to Tara. "Yours?"

"I... never thought about it. I suppose so."

"Long story short, the moon is where the rest of the group locked up Thanatos, the god of death," Colt said.

"Okay." Selene sighed and glanced up to the dark sky. "What time does the moon rise?"

"Eight fifty-one," Tara and Colt replied at the same time.

"What is it we expect to happen, exactly?" Colt asked.

"Darkness will fall," Tara said, causing a shiver to race through Selene.

She was darkness. Maybe what everyone had actually

seen was her death? Maybe she was supposed to somehow sacrifice herself to save everyone. Would she be able to do it? Hell, yes. Hadn't she known from a young age that she didn't belong here. Maybe things would be better if she wasn't there.

"Is that what you've seen?" Selene asked.

"Yes, you?" Tara asked her.

"Not... exactly," Selene answered slowly. "I've seen several things, all ending in a flash of bright light. Like an explosion." That was the truth. For over a year now, she'd come to believe the world ended in light. That somehow, she'd been put here to block that light. To extinguish it.

"That could be— " Tara started, but then a wave of power overtook them both, and they tensed and turned towards the sky.

"Something's wrong," they said together and then everything went dark.

CHAPTER FOUR

"What the hell?" Scott said, looking around him.

"Somnum," a woman said, motioning to him. Instantly, everything went black.

The next thing he could remember was hearing a woman scream. The sound echoed in the empty space.

"What happened?" the blonde asked after light shot out of her fingertips.

That must be Selene's sister, Scott thought vaguely as he sat up. He'd worried that his suit would be ruined from the water at the base of the silo. Instead, it was dry and clean as if he hadn't been lying on the dirty ground moments earlier.

"Hell, if I know," someone said.

"Tara?" Selene asked, sitting up herself. "Did we win?"

"We did," another woman answered. "You might want to go try and explain to your friend why he's in Hidden Creek instead of Atlanta." The woman motioned towards him.

Selene's gaze moved towards him, and her eyes opened wide for a moment before she frowned.

"Scott? How..." she started to ask. "What happened?"

"I'm tired," a dark-haired woman said, getting everyone's attention. "Why don't we head back to our place and fill everyone in on how we bargained to save the world?" Scott thought he heard her mumble, "This time," under her breath.

Selene made her way over to him and took his hand in hers, as if willing him to not run away.

He figured he'd stick around and hear what the hell had just happened to him.

From what he could figure out during the trek back to a large plantation-style home was that he was now in Hidden Creek.

Selene didn't say anything to him, but the looks she was giving him assured him that she felt comfortable here. He'd never seen her like this before—comfortable around a group of people.

Introductions were made quickly, and he tried to keep who was who clear in his mind.

"What do you remember?" the guy named Colt asked. He was apparently with Tara, Selene's sister.

"The three of us were standing in the field together. Then Selene and I mentioned that something didn't feel right. The next thing I remember, you were standing over us," Tara explained.

"That's it?" Colt asked her.

"What happened?" Tara asked.

He sort of tuned out as they all chatted and told their stories. That was until he heard one of the women speak up.

"The witch trumps a god every time," the woman named Jess said with a smile.

Witch? Was she saying she was a witch?

"My wife came up with the plan to call the... your

parents. We all knew they were both going to double-cross you," Jacob said.

"It was sort of obvious. You can't trust a god. Ever," Joleen added. "So while Brea brought Colt to the silo, Joe went and got Scott here." She motioned towards him, and everyone turned to look at him as if they had just realized he was standing there, in the corner of the room, listening in on the very strange conversation.

"Who are..." Colt asked him.

"Scott Logan," Scott supplied, unsure of what else to say.

"My... a friend," Selene added, putting a hand on his arm.

"We grew up together," Scott added, needing to clarify for some odd reason. He'd stopped thinking of Selene as his sister that night almost a year ago when... he stopped the memory from coming and tried to focus on the now.

"I knew that the only way to call on the gods was to pull the two of you, Tara and Selene, from them. The spell I used to do that needed the people closest to the two of you," Jess supplied.

"What happened?" Selene asked.

"Your parents came. They overtook you and were prepared to drag you away to consume your... well, you, I guess." Liz shrugged. "No matter what future I saw, I knew that if they took you, everything would end. Whether in darkness or in light, every world in existence was doomed."

"So we rescued you," Xtina added.

"How?" Tara asked.

"We made a bargain with them. A sleeping god in exchange for the two of you," Jess answered. "For now."

"Why us?" Selene asked.

"Yin and yang," Liz answered. "Lightness." She

motioned towards Tara. "And darkness." She nodded towards Selene. "The same reason the two of you are more powerful together than apart. You are balance."

Scott ran his eyes over Tara. He could easily see that the woman was Selene's complete opposite. Had this group of strangers really just vanquished two gods, as they claimed they had? Whatever had just happened, he needed time alone with Selene to figure it out. To see how much she knew about these people and how much she trusted them.

"What about you?" Xtina asked Selene. "Your parents mentioned that the two of you"—she glanced at Tara as well —"would have more battles. Will you stick around here? Let us help you through whatever is coming?"

Selene glanced over at him. He stared back at her as if not understanding the question.

"I... have some loose ends to tie up first," Selene said, turning away from him. "If there's a place for me here..."

"We're moving into a two-bedroom apartment tomorrow," Tara jumped in.

"And opening a restaurant. If you need a job?" Colt offered.

"Then I suppose I'll be back after," Selene answered slowly, totally surprising him.

He frowned at that. Was she really willing to move here? To be close to these people she'd known for only a handful of hours. Why?

Selene turned to another woman and asked, "If you can see ahead, is that the right choice?"

"It is." The woman turned to him. "For the both of you."

Scott tensed. Were they trying to tell him that he was going to move here? Why? His life was in Atlanta. What the hell would he do in Hidden Creek?

"Thanks," Selene said with a nod. "I think I'll take Scott back to Atlanta."

Selene stood up and walked to the door, and Scott followed her. He wanted to get out of there. Needed to talk to her alone.

"It was... interesting meeting everyone," Scott said, and then he followed Selene outside.

Instead of heading to her car right away, she stood on the porch and wrapped her arms around herself. She was still wearing pretty much the same outfit that she'd worn the other day—dark pants, a band T-shirt, and a leather jacket.

He stood next to her and waited for her to start explaining what in the hell had just happened to him. To her. Just who those people were inside and why they seemed to mean a lot to her suddenly.

When she took a deep breath and reached for his hand, he took it and followed her to her car. The moment she started driving away, she finally spoke.

"I'm sorry you got dragged into this. Were you in a meeting?" she asked, glancing over at him.

It was then that he realized he was still in his suit. Hell, he hadn't even changed.

"I had just gotten home. I was coming after you," he admitted.

She jerked her head towards him. "Dressed like that?"

"No, I... I requested the next week off. I was going to leave when I got home."

"It's after midnight," she pointed out.

"Yeah, I had a... job." He shook his head.

She was quiet for a moment. "So you finished your job first and then you were going to drive to Hidden Creek after midnight?" she asked slowly.

"Yes."

"Why?"

"Because you wouldn't return my damn text messages or calls," he said, getting slightly frustrated.

Instead of pointing the car out of town, she pulled into a parking lot of a hotel. When she parked, he expected her to explain that she was just getting her things. Instead, she turned off the car and turned to him.

"Do you mind crashing here with me tonight? I'm far too tired to drive for a couple hours."

He realized that she did look drained. Normally, she had more energy than anyone he'd ever known. All her life she was like a bubble bouncing around. Now, she looked as if her eyes were on the verge of closing.

"Sure," he said, wishing he had anything of his own. His cell phone was back in his apartment right next to his wallet and keys, which he'd set on the table by his entryway when he'd gotten home.

He followed her into her hotel room, figuring he could shut down for a few hours himself. He had a lot of questions, but it was a long ride back to Atlanta and he'd have plenty of time to ask.

It wasn't until she shut the door behind him that he remembered the last time they'd slept under the same roof.

It had been a year ago, when she'd shown up in the middle of the night at his place during a storm. All those feelings he'd had for her had consumed him.

It had taken all of his strength to make that simple move the night of her sixteenth birthday. Even though it was just a kiss, there were no words to express what it had meant to him. What it still did. Since the rejection of that night, he'd promised himself he would never allow his feelings for her to get the better of him again.

.   .   .

"The moon was falling," Selene had said when he'd opened the door to her.

She had looked sexy as hell with the wet T-shirt she was wearing clinging to her curves. Her long dark hair was in a braid, lying over her shoulder. He wanted to feel all of it tangled in his fingers as he pushed his tongue into her. As he pushed into her. To feel her warm skin next to his. "Falling?" he had asked.

She had wrapped her arms around herself and looked more scared than he'd seen her before. That vulnerability almost broke him. "Yes, it was... massive. It was heading directly towards me. I... felt its power growing in me. It was..." Her eyes closed.

In all his years of knowing her, he'd never remembered seeing her so frightened. He had pulled her close and wrapped his arms around her, only meaning to soothe her. But then she'd shocked him by reaching up, cupping his face, and laying her lips hungrily over his. It was like a shot of adrenaline. The instant pull. The want. Everything that had been dormant burst free.

How long had he hidden it from her?

"Selene," he said, trying to grasp anything normal. It would always be as if his head was in the clouds, as if he had no control, when she was around.

"Scott, for tonight, let's live as if there's no tomorrow," she said, looking up at him as tears slipped from her eyes. "Because I'm not too sure there will be. Please." She'd reached up and kissed him again, her lips hungrily moving over his.

He had been powerless to deny her, mainly since he'd wanted this for as long as he could remember. That first kiss on her sixteenth birthday had rocked him. Until she'd pushed away from him and looked as if she'd just seen a ghost.

Now, however, she was plastering her body next to his while her hands ran over his skin. He'd answered the door in nothing but boxer briefs, while she remained fully clothed in a wet T-shirt and jeans.

"Selene," he groaned when her fingernails scraped against his skin as she lowered her hand to his stomach.

"I've wanted to do this for years," she said against his neck. Then she ran her lips down his chest, licking his skin as she went.

Damn it, he was losing control, and she was dragging him under. Then she jerked away and in a quick motion, removed her wet shirt and toed off her boots. When she reached for the zipper of her jeans, he stopped her.

His mouth had watered during her quick striptease, but there was no way he was going to let her just strip naked. Not yet at any rate.

Taking her hands, he led her through the mess of his living room and into his bedroom. Here, at least, there was some sense of cleanliness.

When he ran a fingertip gently over the rise of her breast, she moaned and threw her head back. She responded so amazingly to him, he had to have more.

He dipped a finger under the black lace of her bra and saw her eyes darken when he circled her nipple. Her skin was so soft and milky white, he had to dip his head for a taste.

"You taste as good as you look," he'd said against her nipple, then he'd sucked it deep into his mouth.

"My god," she'd moaned, tangling her fingers in his hair as he removed her bra completely. "I've always loved your curly hair," she said, holding him against her chest.

"I've always loved your jet-black hair." He reached up and pulled the hair scrunchy he'd given her on her sixteenth birthday from her hair. She put it on her wrist, then smiled as he undid the braid.

She stood in front of him in black jeans, her long dark hair flowing down to her waist, slightly covering her perfect breasts, and he knew she was exactly what she'd claimed she was all her life. She was a goddess.

Without another word, he'd walked to her and stripped her jeans off her body, which took longer than he'd hoped, since they were still wet from the rain. Then he tore off her black silk panties and buried his face into her pussy as she cried out and exploded against his mouth.

He had to have more. Had to fill her. Mark her somehow as his.

He lifted her and laid her gently on the bed and covered her body with his own. When he kissed her again, he slid into her and stilled.

"What the hell?" He frowned down at her as he felt the barrier break free.

"Don't be so surprised," she said as her nails dug into his shoulders. "It doesn't hurt. Don't you dare stop now," she growled as she wrapped her legs around his hips.

He had been surprised but figured they'd have plenty of time to talk about it. Later.

CHAPTER FIVE

Selene closed and locked the hotel room door behind Scott as a wave of desire rushed through her. The last time they'd been alone like this, she'd given herself to him and had been left raw and more hurt than she'd ever been in her life.

She tried to push those memories aside as she sat down to remove her boots.

"So, are you going to tell me what's really going on?" Scott asked as he leaned against the door.

"I would think that would be obvious," she said without looking at him. "We just saved the world." She frowned as she set her boots aside. "Or rather, they did while we apparently were out."

"I mean"—he straightened and walked over to sit next to her—"between us."

"There is no us." She started to stand up, but he stopped her.

"I didn't mean to hurt you," he said softly. "I had just..." He took a deep breath. "You should have warned me you..."

"Were a virgin?" she blurted out. "Did you really think

any man would want to have sex with someone who made all their nightmares play like a movie in their heads while they touched me?" She jerked her hands free and started pacing across the floor. "You had to have known."

When he remained silent, she jerked around to look at him.

"I guess part of me did," he said, looking down at his hands.

Suddenly, she was even more tired than she'd been when she suggested they stay there for the night instead of driving back to Atlanta.

Rubbing her arms, she watched him. "Was it really that bad?" she asked as her chest started hurting.

His head jerked up and his gaze locked with hers. "What? The sex?" he asked, looking slightly shocked. "Hell no. It wasn't..." He shook his head, then surprised her by walking over to her and wrapping his arms around her. "My god, it's all I can do to stop myself from having you again right now. I've thought of nothing since. Haven't been with anyone else since that night." He leaned back and looked into her eyes. "You ruined me," he said with a slight smile. "From the moment I opened my door twenty years ago, it's always been you."

Then he leaned his head down and brushed his lips against hers so softly, so gently, that she felt her soul melt. Her arms wrapped around him, holding him as if he'd vanish in the moments following.

"Selene, I'm sorry I let things end the way they did last year," he said into her hair.

Tears slipped from her eyes. "My entire life has been a lie," she said, looking up into his blue eyes.

"It has?" He frowned down at her.

"I believed nothing could hurt me," she said. When he

understood her meaning, he wiped her tears away with his thumb and then kissed her again.

"I never meant to hurt you," he said softly, then he lifted her in his arms, much like he had a year ago.

This time when he laid her down on the bed, he stood over her, his eyes slowly scanning her until she felt her entire body heat from the want.

"Scott." She reached for him.

"We were in such a hurry last time," he pointed out.

"Who says I'm not in a hurry now?" She leaned up and took his hand.

"This time, I promise I won't say something to make you run out on me in the middle of the night." He knelt beside her and kissed her.

She remembered last time. Remembered being hurt by his words. How he had been unhappy that she hadn't warned him she was still a virgin.

In truth, she hadn't run out on him because of his words. She'd run out on him because it had been too painful not to. The fear of losing him, of losing everything, had been a burden she hadn't wanted him to carry.

Pushing those thoughts to the back of her mind, now that the end of the world had been cancelled, she poured everything she felt for him into the kiss while she unbuttoned his shirt, removed his tie, and basically pawed her way around his sexy body.

Last time, she'd been too shy or too eager to really explore his body. This time, however, after a year of playing that night over in her head a million times, she took what she wanted.

She ran her tongue over every inch of his exposed skin and used her fingertips to make him moan her name. When she wrapped her fingers around his cock, he hissed and dug his fingers into her hips, and she smiled. She was straddling him. They had removed all their clothes, and her long hair was covering her breasts along with his hands.

"You've been thinking about paying me back. Haven't you?" he groaned.

"Yes." She laughed and then lowered her mouth to run the tip of her tongue over his length.

"Damn it," he growled and in one quick move, he spun her until she was flat on the bed with him hovering over him.

Instead of settling between her legs, he straddled her hips, much like she had just been doing to him. It was his turn to run his mouth over her. When he sucked first one, then the other of her nipples into his mouth, she arched for him.

It was even better than she remembered. His hands moved over her hips, lower, until he brushed a fingertip across her pussy. She couldn't stop herself from exploding and crying out his name.

"I've hardly touched you," he said next to her ear.

"Oh god," she moaned as he slipped a finger into her, and she felt even more warmth spread throughout her entire body.

"How many times do you think I can make you come in one night?" he asked as he took her nipple into his mouth while his finger slid in and out of her.

She shook her head and closed her eyes, willing her body back under her control. Then his mouth moved down, trailed over her stomach, until his lips brushed against her clit, and she exploded again.

"That's two," he said with a chuckle. When his tongue darted into her pussy, she cried out for a third time. "More," he growled as his tongue and fingers continued to please her. His tongue flicked over her clit while his fingers brushed against her pussy and her ass, then dipped inside both, and she cried out again.

Then he was covering her, spreading her legs wide and sliding into her.

"Tell me you like this," he demanded.

"Yes," she said, sounding breathless.

"Tell me you want more," he said against her mouth.

"More," she begged. She would have promised him anything. Begged for anything. Given him anything. If he would just keep touching her.

"Selene," he said, stilling for a moment. Her eyes opened and focused on him. "I want you to know it's me inside you."

"Yes, please, Scott." She dug her nails into his hips, willing him to move again.

Then he smiled and started moving again, this time faster, his mouth covering her moans. She wrapped her legs behind his hips, crossing her ankles and holding onto him. When he reached down and ran a fingertip over her nipple, she cried out again, and felt him stiffen over her. Heard him say her name before he collapsed on top of her.

Her entire body shook, vibrated in waves. She hadn't felt this good the last time. She'd had her release, but nothing like this.

It was better than flying. Better than... well, anything she'd experienced before. Sure, she'd experimented with touching herself. After all, she had felt the needs. But nothing came even close to having Scott's hands on her.

"Are you okay?" he asked as he shifted until they were lying side by side with her tucked against him.

"Yes. You?" She glanced back at him.

"Better than okay." He smiled as his hands started

making circles on her stomach. "I'd be even better if you tell me that you have something to eat here."

She smiled and rolled away from him, then walked over to the mini fridge, pulled out the snacks she'd purchased earlier, and brought them a bag of chips, a bag of cookies, and a couple of sodas.

"Road trip food," he said, sitting up. "While we're naked." He took the soda from her.

She sat back down and then reached and tossed him her bra. "If you have to wear something." She smiled as he laughed.

She wasn't self-conscious of her body. Even though this was basically the second time anyone other than her was seeing it, she knew what she had and knew he liked it.

She filled him in on everyone she'd met in Hidden Creek—what their powers were and, most importantly, that they had been the ones to save the world over a year ago when she'd seen the moon fall.

She told him about Xtina. About Jess being a witch. Everything. As she talked, her tone was filled with excitement.

Scott was smiling back at her when she finished the story.

"What?" she asked when he just gave her a look.

"You finally found your people," he said, pulling her into his arms.

She tensed and thought about what he was saying. Yes, for the first time in her life, she felt like she could connect to a group of people. But there was something deeper to this. The only person she truly felt a connection to was him.

"You are my people," she said as she rested her head against his shoulder and relaxed. "Did you really take the week off?"

"Yes," he said, running his fingers gently over her shoulder. "What happens now? Are you really going to move here?"

She thought about the shit apartment and job she had back in Tennessee.

"Yes," she said eagerly. "There's nothing really for me outside of this. Besides, I'd kind of like to see where this all goes."

He was quiet for a while and then surprised her by saying, "Then how about we head up to Tennessee tomorrow? I'll help out for the week."

She glanced up at him. "Really?"

He smiled and leaned his head down to kiss her. "Yeah. Now, let's get some rest. We'll have to stop off at my place and get my stuff. Wallet, phone, and some clothes." He pulled her back down. "Then I'll help you move."

Falling asleep in Scott's arms wasn't anything new to her. But waking up, naked, her body plastered to his was. As was the heated desire for a repeat of last night. But first, she had to use the bathroom. She rolled slowly out of bed, grabbed her T-shirt and a clean pair of underwear, and tiptoed into the bathroom. She shut the door quietly behind her.

After using the toilet, she washed her hands and face and stared at herself in the mirror. Did she look any different?

After yesterday, all of her fears about the end were gone. They had survived the end of the world, and no one had gotten hurt. No one had died. No one...

She heard a deep chuckle and froze. Her reflection in the mirror disappeared. Darkness replaced it. Then slowly, a pair of yellow glowing eyes appeared. They were moving closer to her from the deep.

Her first thought was that her father, Typhon, was back. The man often appeared to her in a giant snake form. But then she realized the yellow eyes weren't slits like on a snake. Instead, they were attached to a man. An extremely handsome man. His jet-black hair was long and slicked back. His square chin had a light dusting of stubble. He was tall, but nothing like the giant her father appeared to be when he was in his human form.

This man was dressed in a very expensive suit, much like the ones that Scott wore.

When she looked down at herself, she realized she was no longer in the hotel bathroom. No longer in her Kiss T-shirt and underwear. Instead, she stood in the darkness in a long flowing dress. Her hair lay over her shoulders in long perfect ringlets.

It made her wonder if his suit was a trick as well. She knew that when she traveled to the Beyond, she could imagine whatever she wanted to wear. She could even conjure weapons if she needed them.

He tilted his head slightly, as if assessing her as much as she was gauging him. Then he smiled at her with perfectly white teeth, and she could see a glimmer of what lay beneath the man.

"We finally meet," he said in a deep voice. "Hello, sister."

CHAPTER SIX

S cott rolled over and when he felt the empty cold spot where Selene should be, he sat up.

"Selene?" he called out. He pulled on his pants and made his way to the bathroom. He knocked first, but when she didn't respond, he opened the door.

She stood in front of the mirror in a T-shirt and underwear. At first, he thought everything was okay, but then he noticed that her eyes were completely white.

He rushed to her, taking her up in his arms and calling her name over and over.

He'd never seen her in a trance like this. He'd seen a few people react this way when she touched them, but never her.

He shook her, called out her name, did anything he could to break her of the spell. Finally, he carried her into the bedroom and laid her down on the bed.

Her body was stiff, as if she was frozen in place.

He waited, checked the time, thought about calling the group from last night. But he didn't even know if Selene had their numbers in her phone. Hell, he didn't even have his phone.

Then he decided to do what he could. He started videotaping her. Stood over her while she was... somewhere else. He didn't know why it was important to video her, but something told him that she would want to know what had happened to her while she'd been... away.

She had talked to him about the place she called the Beyond. He'd watched her disappear and reappear many times over the years. She had even tried to bring him along with her when she disappeared. Each time, he'd end up standing alone.

Disappearing into a different realm was just one of her powers, along with flying, being extremely strong, never getting hurt or sick, and that thing that happened when anyone else touched her. Everyone, except him.

Almost half an hour later, Selene's eyes fluttered and closed before opening again. When she realized he was sitting beside her, her phone aimed at her, she sat up.

"I just met my brother," she said, leaning back on the pillows.

"Great," he said, shutting off the camera. "You have a sister and a brother now?"

"Apparently." She shifted her knees up and hugged them.

"Is that why you went all..." he motioned to her eyes.

She frowned. "I went... what did it look like?"

Instead of answering, he pulled up the video and showed her. She frowned as she watched the few minutes that he had recorded. "That's just... strange." She said, shaking her head and handing him back the phone.

"What did he want? Why wasn't he a part of what happened last night?" he asked.

She glanced towards the window as thunder sounded. "Why don't we pack up and get on our way? We can grab some food on the road, and I'll tell you everything."

"Sure." He leaned in and kissed her, needing this slight touch. She'd scared him. If she had been with anyone else, she would have ended up in the hospital. He poured all of his fears into the kiss, and when she pulled him down on top of her, he willingly went.

How long had he denied his feelings for her? Since he'd first seen her. There was something to the idea that everyone'd had last night. They were connected. The more he touched her, the more he felt it growing.

This time, when he slid into her, he knew there was no doubt his life in Atlanta was over. He couldn't let her go again. It would break him.

They stopped by the donut shop and grabbed a couple of coffees and kolaches and ate as she drove them out of town.

He waited until she was done eating to ask her to start on the story.

"His name is Helios," she said, glancing at him. "But he says that he goes by Lucas." She shrugged.

"Okay," he said slowly. "Wait." He reached over and grabbed her phone. "Like, seriously? You are all a part of Greek mythology. All of you. Even Tara." He frowned down at the screen. He read as much as he could quickly. "Okay, they got some things right, but a lot wrong. You've never been Zeus' lover, have you?" He glanced over at her.

She laughed. "I've only had one lover." Her smile slipped. "Unless you're Zeus." She shook her head. "No."

He smiled. "If I was a god"—he reached over and took her hand while she steered with the other— "I would have definitely saved you from that mess myself."

"Right. My parents didn't seem too interested in you and Colt, other than the fact that we were fated."

He set her phone down. "So what did your brother want?"

"To talk. He was, much like me, unaware of us until last night."

"Does that mean he's going to visit Tara too?"

"No." Selene shook her head. "I asked him not to. Yet. Besides, he told me I'm the one he needs." She was frowning.

"Needs?" He watched her closely. "For what?"

"A ride, basically."

"To?" He knew her well enough to understand she was still trying to process things and trying to keep him from freaking out at the answer.

"Hell," she said softly. So softly that he almost missed it.

"What?" He shifted to get a better look at her.

"The Beyond. It's... hell," she said a little louder.

He thought for a moment then busted out, "The place you've been going to all your life, the place you use as your..."—he air quoted— "you time, is actually hell?" He was practically screaming now.

"Apparently." She shrugged.

He turned back around and looked out the side window until he got his breathing under control. "What did you tell him?"

"No," she said quickly.

He turned back to her. "Why not?"

"Because my brother wants to wake the devil." She rolled her eyes.

"He..." At this point, Scott's brain stopped working. Like, how could you even think after someone just told you something like that. It took him a few minutes of silence to get his thoughts back. "Why? Why does Helios, your brother..."

"He goes by Lucas, and we're triplets," she reminded him.

"Okay." He rubbed his forehead. "Why does Lucas want a ride to hell to wake the devil?"

Selene pulled over into a gas station, parked on the side of the building, and shut off the car.

"Because he thinks that by waking him, we can stop the end of the world," she said softly.

"Your brother is going to stop the end of the world by waking the devil?" he asked, not understanding. "Didn't you just save the world from your parents last night?"

"No, I mean, yes, we did. And my brother isn't going to save the world alone." She turned to him. "He says that you have to be there too." He eyes locked with his.

He shook his head. "What?"

"He wants me to take the two of you to hell so he can wake the devil and you can stop him. That is why I said no." She started to get out of the car, but reached over and held her still.

What she was saying was impossible in so many ways. First, hell. Second, if he traveled to hell, wouldn't that mean he was dead? Third, how was he supposed to stop the devil? He didn't have powers like Selene and the rest of her family and new friends. He was just... Scott. Boring, office-working Scott.

"There's more to it, isn't there?" he asked, feeling tired.

"Yes, but right now, I need to pee." She climbed out of the car.

He watched her walk into the store, waited for her to come back out. But after she used the bathroom, she strolled down the aisle and grabbed a bag of chips and a couple of candy bars. For as long as he'd known her, she'd loved junk food.

She was standing in line to pay when a large man dressed in black rushed in. He'd been paying so much attention to Selene that he hadn't noticed the guy until the gun was shoved in the clerk's face.

Just as he reached for the door handle to run in and help, Selene gripped the man's wrist. Within seconds, the man was on his knees. The gun flew from his hands as he cried out in pain.

The clerk had ducked behind the counter the moment the gun had appeared.

While the man continued to cry on the floor, Selene set some money on the counter, talked briefly to the clerk over the counter, and turned and walked out.

"What..." he said, when she got in and started backing up.

"I wanted to convince the clerk to erase the footage. He said there aren't any cameras." She shrugged. "So we're all good."

He took a deep breath. "That's happened to you before, hasn't it?"

She shrugged again. "I live in the shitty part of town."

How many times over the years had he lectured her about being seen? Then her words hit him.

"Convince the clerk?" He frowned over at her.

She bit her lip and winced. "I... asked."

"No." He shook his head, seeing her lie before she said anything more. "The truth."

She took another deep breath. "Okay, I can convince people to do things, sometimes."

"Sometimes?"

"When I... whisper."

His eyes narrowed. "Does it work on me?"

She shook her head quickly, and he knew she was telling the truth. "Nothing I do works on you."

"Except that time that you took me flying," he pointed out.

She smiled. "Right." Then she laughed. "I've never seen you more afraid in your life."

"You almost dropped me. On purpose," he pointed out. She was strong enough to keep a hold of him, so he knew she had let go of him on purpose.

"Don't be a baby." She handed him the bag of chips.

He took one and ate it. "How does your brother think I'm going to stop the world from being destroyed?"

She glanced sideways at him. "Who knows."

Again, he could tell instantly that she was lying. "Selene..."

She sighed and threw up one of her hands, then banged it on the steering wheel.

"Something about where you come from," she finally admitted.

"Georgia?" He frowned.

She shrugged. "He didn't say. Only that you were an important key to his plan."

"Which is?"

"Waking the devil and fighting the demons himself." She glanced at him again as she turned off the highway and headed towards his place.

Nothing she was saying made sense, unless you had grown up around Selene and had seen all the strange things she could do. Then it just scared the shit out of you.

What sort of powers did her brother have? Obviously, he couldn't travel to the Beyond like she could, or he'd drag Scott there himself.

She was pulling up in front of his apartment building and suddenly he realized that she knew where his new place was.

He glanced sideways at her.

"You may have lost track of me, but I never lost sight of you." She shut off the engine. "Come on, let's get your stuff."

He followed her up to the top floor, where his two-bedroom penthouse sat overlooking the river. The place was a million times better than the last place he'd had.

The luck he'd had at his job had afforded him the new place and the expensive car he had purchased a few months ago. Finally, things had been going his way. And then Selene had shown up again.

CHAPTER SEVEN

There was little that shocked Selene. But as she looked around Scott's new place, she was speechless.

"This is your place?" she asked for the second time. Scott glanced over his shoulder at her and rolled his eyes.

"Come on, you can help me pack." He headed down the hallway.

She followed him past the massive living room filled with expensive furniture, through a large kitchen, then past a bedroom that he'd turned into a home gym slash office space.

His main bedroom was bigger than the loft apartment she was currently squatting in.

"Remind me what it is you do again?" she asked, turning in circles.

"I handle accounts," he said as he pulled out a suitcase.

"Right." She motioned around the apartment. "It's a hell of a lot cleaner than your last place."

He chuckled. "Yeah, I wasn't in the right headspace last time you stopped by my place."

She ran a finger down one of his suits hanging in the massive walk-in closet. She turned and raised her eyebrows. "As opposed to the space you and the brunette were in when I walked in on you in your office a few days ago?"

"Was that only a few days ago?" He shook his head and walked over and grabbed a few pairs of jeans. "Seems like longer." He set the pants down next to the bag he'd gotten and then wrapped his arms around her. "You know, we could always move your stuff here."

She felt her entire body warm at that thought. Hadn't she wanted to be with him like this her entire life?

As tempting as it was, she couldn't deny the calling she felt to be with her new friends and, most importantly, to be in Hidden Creek. Even though the danger was over, temporarily, she could feel something else brewing. Something... different than before. She needed time and a trip to the Beyond to figure things out. She knew neither of those were possible as long as Scott was around.

Once he had changed into a pair of worn jeans and a black T-shirt, he tossed a few things into a backpack and grabbed his wallet and phone. Then they headed out again, only this time he suggested they take his car instead of hers.

She didn't mind since his car was a shiny new silver BMW with leather seats and a kick-ass satellite radio system, which she played with for the next two and a half hours while they drove up to Tennessee.

Just outside of Chattanooga, they stopped for dinner at one of her favorite barbeque places. She'd never thought she'd move to Chattanooga, but it was closer to Atlanta than Nashville was, so she'd left a high-paying managerial job and headed to the smaller city. It was harder to avoid seeing the same people over and over in a place like Chattanooga. Especially a town where most people didn't trust anyone new, particularly when they dressed and looked like her.

If it was possible, she would have covered herself with tattoos over the years. She'd even tried to learn how to tattoo herself, but the ink never stuck. It was the universe's way of fucking her over in a whole different way.

So she wore black band shirts and leather or black jeans with combat boots. With her dark hair and eyes, most people took one look at her and crossed the street, except for a not insignificant number of men who tried to flirt with her. Maybe they thought she was easy or that she was a bad girl. Either way, if they annoyed her enough, all she had to do was brush her fingers across their skin and they too would go out of their way to avoid her, just like everyone else.

Everyone except Scott. She glanced across the table at him and smiled at the barbeque sauce dripping down his stubbled chin. Thoughts of sucking the sweet and tangy sauce from his skin heated her entire body.

Damn, it was going to be really hard letting him go. She knew in her heart that he wouldn't leave his job and his amazing life in Atlanta. Just one look at his place confirmed that fact.

"You're quiet," he said, wiping the sauce from his face, then taking another sip of his beer.

"The food is good." She took another bite of ribs.

His eyes narrowed, and she knew he understood there was more to it.

"I guess I'm a little nervous about moving to a small town," she admitted.

"Then don't. Move in with me."

She shook her head. "It's not..." She wanted to move in with him. Really, she did. But there were so many answers she needed. "I feel like it's the right move for now."

He nodded slowly. "Yeah, I figured. You seem pretty determined. I know better than to step in your way when you're that sure about anything." He smiled, and she felt the familiar flutter in her gut that his smile had always caused.

"You could come with to Hidden Creek?" she suggested.

He looked down at his hands and shrugged. "Let's get your stuff first and see what happens."

Selene's one-room loft apartment was nothing much to look at. Over the years she had jumped from one hole-in-the-wall to another. She had picked up some of the used furniture that filled the small space at a second-hand store, but most of it she'd found on the side of the road or in a dumpster and had refurbished herself.

Compared to his place, hers looked like a dump. Even though she was clean, almost compulsive about it, the four-hundred-square-foot place looked... well... dumpy. Her mismatched, brightly colored furniture had seen better days.

Leaving Scott standing by the door, she walked into her bedroom and started packing up her personal items. She would have to arrange with the building manager to have the furniture donated or just hauled away.

"Are you going to be moving all of this?" he asked, following her back through the curtain she had hung to separate the living spaces.

"No, just my clothes and personal things. I'll donate the rest." She shrugged as she started putting her clothes into her luggage. "This shouldn't take me long."

"We can head back to Atlanta and stay at my place? We should get back around dinnertime," he suggested, sitting on the side of her bed.

She glanced over at him as she pulled a stack of socks

from her drawer. "Sure," she said, trying not to let her voice reflect the fact that her heart had practically leapt out of her chest at the thought of repeating what had happened the night before.

It took a couple trips to get her things down and into the trunk of his car. The fact that everything that mattered to her fit in the trunk of his car slightly depressed her.

Not that she was a material sort of person. She liked having few enough belongings that she could pack up and move all by herself. Didn't she?

After leaving a message for Larry, the building manager, she locked the door and slid the key under it before walking away without looking back.

"You did that so casually," Scott said as he drove away.

"It was a shithole," she said with a slight shrug.

"Yeah, but still, it was home for a while." He glanced sideways at her. "I remember every time we moved as kids. You used to be more sentimental."

"We're not kids anymore."

He was silent for a while. "Still, I doubt I could fit everything I have in the trunk of a car."

She glanced over at him, then nudged his arm. "Diva."

He laughed at the old joke they used to share whenever they had to leave something sentimental behind.

As they made their way back to Atlanta, they talked about their childhood together. They tried to figure out how many different homes they'd been in, but they couldn't agree.

When she tried to prod him further on his new job, he acted slightly embarrassed and tried many times to change the subject. But she stuck to her guns and shortly before they arrived back at his place, she got some information from him.

"I handle accounts," he said at one point.

"You already said that. I thought the company you worked for was in marketing of some sort?"

"Of sorts," he answered.

"Scott, are you being obscure on purpose?" She narrowed her eyes at him.

He finally sighed and relented a little. "We handle large accounts. Multi-billion-dollar accounts. We market people and their personae or businesses."

"Like... movie stars?"

"Yes, we have some as our clients." He nodded.

"Okay, so you what? Help them market themselves?"

"Sometimes."

She growled. "Seriously? Your entire life is an open book to me, yet you can't tell me what it is you do each day?" She threw up her hands.

"I signed contracts agreeing not to talk about what I do and who I do it for."

"Sure, to anyone else, but I'm..." She stopped herself from saying the word *sister*. They weren't related. Sure, they'd grown up together, but there had always been something more between them. She couldn't even bring herself to say the word *family*. Their bond went beyond even that construct. "Selene," she finished after a brief delay.

Scott chuckled. "Okay, I won't be able to divulge any names, but what I can tell you is that our clients depend on us to keep what we do for them secret. My list of clients includes a couple of movie stars you like and one you don't, a few musicians that you definitely love, a couple of politicians, and"—he smiled over at her—"an author whose books you have read so many times."

This was going to kill her. As he pulled back into his

parking garage, she started listing off names. Each time as an answer, he only chuckled and shook his head.

"I'll get one of the names from you," she warned as she pulled out her overnight bag from the back seat of his car.

"You can try," he joked as he took the bag from her. "But I'd wager..."

The moment their hands touched, his eyes faded slightly, and he stilled. Hell, he froze in place. Her first thought was to jerk her hand away, thinking that somehow, after all this time, she'd finally had an effect on him.

Only, his eyes didn't go completely white. Instead, they just... went blank.

"Hello," a woman's voice said from behind her, causing her to jump. "I didn't mean to scare you."

Selene turned to see an Asian woman roughly her age walking towards her. The first thing Selene noticed was that she was beautiful. Like, knock-your-socks-off beauty. Instantly, Selene felt a kick of jealousy, but she squashed it quickly.

The woman's long dark hair flowed past her shoulders. She was dressed in designer clothes, showcasing that she'd grown up with money and style, things Selene had had little of. The woman's dark eyes were filled with curiosity and... something else that had Selene reining in the desire to fight —friendliness.

"Then why don't you release my friend to prove it?" Selene suggested.

The woman glanced over at Scott. "If you are okay with him hearing what it is I want to discuss with you..."

Selene instantly knew that the woman was talking about power. Whatever this woman wanted to talk about, she was kind enough to keep the supernatural part of it away from others.

"He knows who and what I am," Selene said quickly.

The woman ran her eyes over Selene, then moved to Scott and nodded. Instantly, Scott was freed. He finished his sentence as if nothing had happened. "...you won't get too far." He stilled when he noticed Selene had moved and that they were no longer alone.

Selene smiled when he tried to shove her behind him, as if to protect her. A few seconds later, he relaxed.

"Oh, hey, Mia," Scott said casually. "I didn't see you there."

Mia glanced over at Selene, as if waiting for her to say something. Selene put her hand on Scott's arm. "I think your friend wants to have a chat?"

Scott frowned down at her. "What?"

Mia stepped forward. "I felt you arrive earlier," she said, her eyes on Selene. "But now that you're back and... care to sit down for a cup of coffee?"

Scott frowned as Selene nodded. "Sure. How about we put my things up in Scott's apartment and meet you..." She turned to Scott, her eyebrows raised.

"There's a coffee place on the corner," he suggested.

Mia smiled. "I'll see you there in ten." She turned to go but stopped. "I'm Mia by the way."

"Selene," Selene supplied.

Mia's eyes went wide for a split second before she turned and walked away.

"Want to tell me what that was all about?" Scott asked as they started heading up to his apartment.

"She has power. A lot of it," Selene said.

She kicked herself mentally for not feeling it earlier. She'd been too preoccupied with flirting with Scott to feel the crackle in the air. She'd let the woman sneak up on them. What would have happened if it hadn't ended well?

"Mia does?" Scott asked with a frown.

"Yes." Selene sighed and dreamed of a hot shower to wash the day's stink off from sitting in the car for so long.

Instead, she dumped her bag on Scott's sofa and headed out the door to go meet another person with power.

CHAPTER EIGHT

Scott sat next to Selene in the booth, and Mia sat directly across from them.

Even though it was past nine at night, the coffee bar was almost packed. After receiving their orders, Mia glanced at Selene.

"Is it okay if I keep this conversation to the three of us?" Mia asked.

Selene glanced around and nodded.

Mia smiled and, suddenly, everything stopped. The noise in the coffee shop, all movement. Even the air seemed to still.

"There, that's better." Mia relaxed back. "What are you?"

"I'm..." Selene leaned forward, her elbows on the table. "The goddess of darkness. You?"

"Wow, really? A goddess?" Mia looked interested. "There really isn't a name for what I am. The closest label, which has been handed down my family's blood line, is djinn."

"Seriously?" Selene tilted her head, then looked over at him.

"Which means?" he asked with a slight shrug.

Selene smiled. "She's a genie."

He turned to Mia and ran his eyes over her. She'd been living in the apartment complex longer than he had. He'd noticed her the first week after moving in. On several occasions, he'd thought of asking her out, but the timing had never been right.

They'd done some minor flirting, or at least he'd thought they had. Not once during the past year had he thought anything such as this about her.

"A genie? Like in Aladdin?" he asked.

Mia chuckled. "Yes, but I'm not made of blue smoke and can't grant wishes."

"What are your powers? If you don't mind me asking," Selene said.

"Besides this"—Mia waved her hand to the stillness—"one of my favorites is..." In the next seconds, Mia's face transformed. Then her entire body shifted, and her hair seemed to grow everywhere. Seconds later, a very large black dog sat where Mia had been. "I can't keep the form for long, but..." The dog smiled back at them, then started to change back to Mia.

"That is so wicked," Selene practically clapped. "What else?"

Mia smiled. "I showed you one of mine." She motioned to Selene.

Selene frowned and then nodded. "Okay, but mine are a little... darker." She held out her hand. When Mia started to put her hand in hers, Selene pulled back slightly and said, "Don't freak. It's just a vision."

How many times in his life had he seen what happened

to people when they touched Selene? Too many. Watching Mia's eyes go white and the blood drain from her face still got to him.

Mia jerked her hands back and frowned towards Selene. "I can do visions too, but mine are..." She shifted and locked eyes with him.

Instantly, images of him and Selene walking on a beach somewhere filled his mind. Selene was in a ridiculously small black bikini. She had on large black sunglasses, shielding her eyes from him.

"Is this everything you imagined it would be?" she asked him.

He turned to her and wrapped his arms around her. "Yes, and more," he said before kissing her.

"...happy," Mia finished as the images disappeared.

Selene was looking at him as if waiting for him to fill her in on what had just happened.

"Cool trick," he said, squeezing Selene's hand under the table.

"What else can you do?" Mia asked.

"Besides bending light and controlling fire, I can't be hurt. I'm ridiculously strong. Oh, and I can fly," she finished with a smile.

Mia was quiet for a moment. "Wow, okay, that's more than I've got. Stopping time and shapeshifting into a dog—that's pretty much it."

"You mentioned something about your family. Are there any others like you?" Scott asked her.

"Nope. One lucky family member at a time gets to hold the gift." She shrugged. "Usually, it's the oldest child, but after my brother died when he was five, I was granted the powers."

"So it runs in your family?" Selene asked. Her eyes narrowed slightly as if she was thinking.

"Yup, it has for more generations than I can count. We're the stuff legends are made of." She shrugged softly. "There has been folklore about my family since before the Ming dynasty."

"That's... cool." Selene smiled. "Plus, the whole shapeshifter thing."

"Oh please." Mia smiled. "You can fly."

"Yeah, but the chances of someone seeing me makes that gift practically useless." Selene glanced at him briefly.

"Do your powers run in your family?" Mia asked, curious.

"I have a sister who can pretty much do what I do, but she is light, not darkness. My brother..." Selene frowned. "I just found out about him. Other than one power, I have no clue what he can do."

Mia sipped her coffee. "You and Scott..." She nodded between them.

"We grew up together," he said suddenly, then he picked up Selene's hand and showed Mia. "This is a recent progression."

Mia smiled. "You two look good together. I have a knack for spotting love matches."

He felt Selene's hand tense in his.

"There are more of us. I mean, people with powers. We're heading back to Hidden Creek tomorrow."

"Hidden Creek?" Mia frowned. "I read the newspaper articles a while back. I was pretty sure it was all fake. You know how these kinds of things can be exploited and embellished for profit."

"It's true. The group is led by Xtina. I can vouch for the power there. My sister Tara is there." Selene smiled.

"I may have to make a trip there myself soon." Mia nodded.

"Just how long can you halt time for?" Scott asked Mia.

Mia glanced around. "Normally, about half an hour at a time. How long will you be staying with Scott?" she asked Selene, who glanced his direction.

"A few nights. Then we'll head back to get her settled in Hidden Creek," he answered easily. He wanted—no, needed—some time with her.

Suddenly, everything started moving again. The noise in the coffee shop was almost deafening.

"Yup, about half an hour," Mia said with a smile. "I'd like to time it, but..." She held up her watch. "There's no way to."

Scott glanced at his phone and realized Mia's watch showed the same time as his phone.

"That makes me wonder if the Earth stops rotating," he said out loud.

"It does. Everything stops. I can move a few things, but outside of..."—she motioned to her coffee mug—"everything else stays put. I once tried to drive a car. The engine was stopped, and it wouldn't budge. I can ride a bike though."

"Very cool," Selene said. "I have a place I can go," she said, looking down at her hands. "My entire life I've called it the Beyond."

"What kind of place?" Mia asked with a slight frown.

"It's... beyond this plane. To my knowledge, I'm the only one there."

He silently thought about what she'd told him about her brother's thoughts. If Selene's Beyond world was really hell, then wouldn't there be... evil there?

Mia surprised them both by saying. "I call it the Void," she said.

"You can go there?" Selene sat forward.

"Large place, filled with light and sand? Yes." Mia nodded.

"N-no." Selene shook her head. "The Beyond is dark. No sand. There are red flowing rivers, like lava, but not hot. No sun, no light."

Mia frowned. "Maybe they're not the same. I was told that the Void was a safe space. A place to go when I'm in trouble."

"Have you been in trouble before?" Scott asked.

Mia glanced at him. "Last year and a few nights ago," she nodded.

"The moon each time?" Selene asked.

Mia's eyes moved to hers and she nodded. "You saw it too?"

"The people I was telling you about in Hidden Creek. They stopped it. My parents..." Selene shook her head. "Long story, made short. My father is Typhon, father of monsters, and my mother is Rhea, mother of gods. Anyway, they came back to consume Tara and me. But Xtina and her group outwitted them. At least for a while."

"That's good to know," Mia said, relaxing back. "I was in the Void until I felt you return earlier today. I had moved my entire family there, but now that it's safe, I've moved them back."

"Wait, you can take others there?" Selene asked.

"Sure. Can't you take others to your Beyond?" Mia asked.

"No." Selene glanced in his direction. "I've tried. Trust me."

She had. How many times over the years had Selene tried to take him to her magical world? Too many.

"Maybe I can help with that. I was eighteen before I

could take anyone else with me. I had to practice and learn how to do it," Mia said.

"You... learned?" Selene asked. "That would be..." She was silent for a while.

"Helpful," he finished for her. The thought of traveling to the Beyond, or hell, frightened him. But what scared him more was the possibility that he was meant to do something that would save the world and wouldn't be able to.

Selene and Tara had done their part to try and save the world days ago. Soon, it would be his turn. Even if he didn't believe Selene's brother, he couldn't deny that it was a strategic benefit for Selene to learn all that she could.

Besides, this would allow them to spend a little more time in Atlanta. Together.

"I have a wild idea." Mia leaned forward. "Normally, I wouldn't ask strangers, but after..." She shook her head. "How would the two of you like to spend some time at my family's ranch outside of town?"

Selene was quiet for a moment. "I'm supposed to head back to Hidden Creek, but if you're willing to teach me what you can, I'm game." She glanced in his direction when she was done speaking.

"I'm not due back at work for ten days," he chimed in. He'd been saving up all his leave for a trip but had taken it all for Selene.

"Perfect. We can leave in the morning." Mia stood up and looked at him. "I'll knock on your door at a quarter after seven."

After she left, he shifted to get a better look at Selene.

"Thoughts?" he asked.

"On Mia?" Selene relaxed back. "She's the real deal. Powerful. We can trust her."

He didn't ask how she knew that part of it. Their entire

lives, he had never asked any questions after she'd done her magic on anyone, but he knew that when she touched them, they saw their worst nightmares, and she got a glimpse into their souls.

"You don't have to come along if you don't want to." She dropped her hand from his to take a bite of the muffin she'd gotten with her coffee.

He was starving, but since they'd run into Mia, his plans of ordering delivery had been spoiled. Instead, they'd each grabbed a muffin and coffee at the coffee shop.

"No, I'm going." He glanced around. "There's a Thai place across the street. How about we head over there and get some real food?"

"You're buying." She tossed down the rest of the muffin and climbed out of the booth.

CHAPTER NINE

Lying in Scott's bed later that night, listening to his heartbeat against her ear, she thought over the decision she was making. If she learned how to bring others to the Beyond, then wasn't she feeding into her brother's wish to take Scott to the realm?

So far, she hadn't had any visions of what her brother spoke of. For years prior to what had happened in Hidden Creek, she'd dreamed of the world's destruction. In her mind, she'd witnessed the destruction of everything so many ways, she'd lost track of living.

Now she was finally freed of that darkness, and here was a new horror she was forced to face. So why did she feel the pull to go with Mia and learn the one thing that her brother needed for his demands?

Her mind went in circles until she finally drifted off to sleep.

As darkness swirled around her mind, she watched it shift and grow into a form.

"Hello, sister. Thinking of me?" Lucas was lounging on a bed, shirtless, and there were black silk sheets covering his hips. She assumed he was naked underneath. There was a dark figure lying beside him, but she could only see the shape.

"No," she denied, but he shifted and, suddenly, they were somewhere else, both of them fully clothed. They stood on a large balcony overlooking a huge city. It was still night, and she wondered if this was where he really was or if he had just conjured up the location.

"Dreaming then." Lucas smiled. "You're worried about your man." It was a statement, not a question.

"Wouldn't you be worried about whomever I just saw you with if roles were reversed?" she countered.

Lucas' smile shifted. "If you asked me, I wouldn't even be able to tell you her name."

She didn't doubt it. He looked like a player. His jet-black hair was slicked back. His sharp jawline had just the right amount of stubble, and his hazel-yellow eyes no doubt drove many women crazy. He was tall, six-three or six-four. Once again, he was dressed to impress, this time in a black turtleneck and jeans. Even though it wasn't the expensive suit like last time, his attire spoke of wealth. Then again, he could be projecting this image of himself just like he was the location.

"Where are you?" she asked easily.

He tilted his head slightly. "You're back in Atlanta. I'm in New York," he said, and she knew he was telling the truth.

"Why New York?" she asked. "Is that where you've always been?"

"No," he answered. "Is Atlanta home?"

"For now." She crossed her arms over her chest. Last time, she'd been in a long flowing dress. This time, it was a black sweater and jeans. She didn't know if he'd conjured up the outfit or if she had.

"You've thought about our last conversation," he said, leaning against the railing.

"Who wouldn't? You basically told me that Scott has to stop the end of the world by killing the devil." She leaned next to him.

He chuckled. "That's putting it simply."

She raised her eyebrows. "Then please unsimplify it for me." She waved her hand.

His eyes ran over her. "Before the year's end, Scott Logan will wake Moros, also known as the morning star or Phosphorus, Lucifer, and, in some cultures, Hades."

"Okay." Selene started pacing the balcony. "Why? Why him?"

Lucas sighed. "Because he is yours. Because he comes from the same place."

"That's bullshit." She turned on him.

He shrugged. "I didn't make the rules. Because he is with you, he holds even more power."

Her eyes narrowed. "What kind of power?"

Instead of answering, Lucas stood straight and looked at her. Right before her eyes, he shifted, much like Mia had. Only, instead of a cute black-haired dog, Lucas stood before her as a six-foot wolf with pitch-dark hair. His yellow eyes gleamed with both humor and hunger.

As with Mia, when he spoke, his mouth didn't move. Instead, the words filled her mind.

"There are things beyond our comprehension, sister. Learn what you must at the ranch, but know this—before the next full moon, if you don't bring him to me, I'll be forced to take matters into my own hands." With this, blackness swirled around her brother until she could only see his glowing yellow eyes. Then he disappeared.

She woke with a start as sunlight blinded her. Scott stood next to the bed, holding out a mug of coffee.

"Morning." He smiled down at her. "Did you sleep well?"

As an answer, she sipped the coffee in silence.

"I forgot, you're not a morning person." He sat on the edge of the bed. She noticed that he was fully dressed and grunted. "Mia's going to be here in half an hour. I thought you'd like to shower first." She grunted again and he chuckled. "If you go stand under the water, I'll get you a second cup of coffee."

She rolled her eyes and tossed the covers off her naked body. Taking the cup with her, she stood under the spray, letting the hot water wash away the darkness from her dreams.

Had she really visited her brother last night? There was no way her imagination could conjure up all of that.

When Scott's hand appeared between the foggy glass doors of his shower with a fresh cup of coffee, she figured she'd better wash her hair and get ready.

"Thanks," she said, taking it from his hand.

"Do you know how hard it was not to poke my head in there? But," he said with a heavy sigh, "if I did, there would be no way we'd be ready by the time Mia gets here."

She smiled as she rinsed the shampoo from her hair and shut off the water. Taking the full cup of coffee, which she'd set on the glass shelf in the shower, she stepped out. Scott was there, holding up a large white towel for her to step into.

"Feel better?" he asked her.

"Rested," she confirmed. "And eager to get learning.

Something tells me Mia has more than just one thing to teach me."

"She does seem like an old soul," Scott said, leaning against the countertop.

"Do you believe in that stuff?" she asked as she pulled on some clean clothes. His laughter stopped her. "What?"

"After growing up beside you, watching everything you can do, you really need to ask me if I believe in old souls?" His eyebrows rose.

She shrugged. "It's just..." She thought about what she'd learned about herself and Tara. How this hadn't been the first time that their parents had consumed them. Suddenly, she had another question plaguing her. Why them and not Lucas?

Instead of answering, she shook her head and finished dressing, then spent a few minutes trying to tie her long hair back. She'd let it grow out and still had no clue how to make it look like anything other than a rat's nest. Finally, she pulled it up into a messy bun and gulped down the rest of her coffee.

"Breakfast?" he asked, just as a knock sounded on the door. "Guess we'll stop on the way." He shrugged and stepped out of the bathroom.

Sitting on the edge of the massive sunken tub, she pulled on her boots, then grabbed up her overnight bag filled with her necessities and went out to see Scott talking to Mia.

"Ready?" Mia asked with a smile. "I thought we'd hit the bakery downstairs before we hit the road. They have the best sticky buns."

Selene felt her stomach growl at the thought of a sticky bun.

"Sounds good," she said, tossing her bag over her shoulder. Scott's backpack was already over his shoulder.

For good measure, Selene grabbed a sticky bun and a breakfast quiche, as well as an iced coffee for the road.

She sat in the back of Scott's car while Mia gave him directions. They headed out of the city and weaving through the Atlanta traffic actually took up the majority of the trip. The second they hit the open road, Mia had Scott turning off the highway. Another half an hour and they stopped outside of two massive iron gates.

Mia pulled out what looked like a garage door opener and the gates began to open.

"Do your parents live here?" Scott asked as he started up the gravel driveway.

"No, usually they're in New York. This is their winter home, but the last few years they've stayed in the city. They want me to move out here, but..." She shrugged and slowed the car when the gravel path turned into cement.

The home finally came into view. It wasn't massive or new. The single-story ranch appeared very country and quaint. There was wood siding in places and stone everywhere else. The three-car garage had barn doors with wood beams crossing them. They were painted a dark brown.

"You can park here," Mia said, and Scott stopped the car just outside the garages. "There are five bedrooms and bathrooms. Take your pick. My room is at the end of the hall on the left," she pointed out. "There's a pool. If it stays warm, we can enjoy it. If not, there's a firepit. I ordered grocery delivery, which should be here"—she glanced down at her watch—"in half an hour." She got out of the car. "Have a look around, get settled. We'll start training after lunch."

The house didn't look big enough to hold five bedrooms

and bathrooms, but the moment they stepped through the double front doors, Selene realized that the house went on for farther than it seemed from the front. The entire back of the house overlooked a pool, a pond, and a field. It became clear that the place was two stories with the main floor being the top floor.

"There are three bedrooms downstairs." Mia motioned to a set of stairs with an iron railing.

They had each grabbed their own bags, and they watched Mia disappear down a hallway, leaving them to explore the house.

The entryway forced them to either follow Mia down a hallway or turn to the left and enter a large living room that connected to the kitchen. A set of stairs separated the entry and the space. Selene could see a massive deck off the back of the house, where rocking chairs and recliners sat overlooking the pool and pond.

"Want to head downstairs?" Scott suggested.

"Sure," she said, following him down. They stepped into a living space that had a massive pool table and was attached to a smaller kitchen.

She followed Scott down a short hallway and, when he opened a door, they both looked into a darkened home theater.

"Wow, I've always wanted a home theater," Scott said.

"I like falling asleep on a couch too much," she pointed out as she opened another door and looked in on a half-bathroom. He followed her down the long hallway on the other side of the stairs.

Here, they looked in on three unique bedrooms. In the end, they settled on a big room with an amazing tiled bathroom that had a shower big enough for an entire football team and a bathtub she drooled over.

After putting their bags on the king-sized bed, they headed back up the stairs and heard Mia talking to the grocery delivery person.

Scott helped the teenager carry in the rest of the bags as Selene helped Mia put things away. She wanted to ask Mia how long they planned on staying, since there was enough food here to last a month but decided to just be thankful that it appeared Mia had the same tastes Selene did.

She put a few bags of her favorite potato chips away in the walk-in pantry along with cereal and other snack foods. There was enough meat to practically fill the massive double refrigerator, everything from steaks to fresh salmon.

There were even bagels and cream cheese and some other breakfast foods.

"You thought of everything," she said to Mia.

"Believe it or not, this is the standard grocery order we get when the entire family comes home." Mia chuckled. "With a few additions." She held up the bottle of whiskey. "I know Scott likes this brand."

Selene frowned. "You do?" Suddenly, she wondered just how well Scott knew Mia. They did live in the same building, after all. Had they gone out or slept together?

"It's another one of my gifts. I forgot to mention it earlier," Mia said with a shrug. "It's also how I knew what brand of shampoo to get you." She held up a bottle.

Sure enough, it was Selene's favorite brand of shampoo and conditioner. Mia had even gotten Scott his favorite brand of aftershave.

"It's freaky, having her know all these things about us, but at the same time, it's not," Scott said as they took the bag of their things downstairs to put away in their room. "You know, I can't remember anymore a time when things like this seemed odd to me."

She smiled and said, "I know what you mean." But had there ever been a time where she hadn't thought she was strange? That there was something wrong with her?

What had it been like for Mia to grow up in a loving family where her abilities were not shunned but praised and celebrated?

That thought stayed with her the entire time the three of them made sandwiches and ate lunch out on the back deck. Today it was a little chilly, so she'd grabbed one of her sweatshirts, and Mia had lit the firepit that sat on the deck.

"Tomorrow it's supposed to be warmer," Mia assured them. "But if you want, the hot tub is directly under us on the porch."

Scott glanced over at her and wiggled his eyebrows. "Nice," he said, nudging her knee.

She remembered the last time they'd been in a hot tub together. They had snuck into the apartment complex across the road from one of their foster homes. They hadn't gotten caught, but she'd ended up throwing up the cold pizza they'd eaten beforehand.

"Great," she said less enthusiastically.

"So what's the deal with you two?" Mia asked, kicking up her bare feet and resting them near the fire. "I get that you're an item now. You were raised together?"

"Foster care." Scott nodded. "Selene was six. After that, we were inseparable. I think I was drawn to the thrill and excitement of the things she can do from the first moment I saw her powers."

Selene was surprised at this. She'd never really talked to Scott about these sorts of things. She'd always assumed he'd felt the same way she had from the moment they had seen one another.

"It must have been nice being raised to know exactly

what you were," Selene broke in, a little uncomfortable with the topic.

"Yes and no. Constantly being compared to your ancestors and their powers has a downside." Mia shrugged. "Oh, you can't levitate? Your great-great-aunt could," she said in a somewhat whiney tone. "What do you mean you can't command the weather? Your great-great-great-grandfather could." She rolled her eyes.

"Seriously?" Scott asked, leaning forward slightly.

Mia chuckled. "Yes, djinns are known for their power and abilities, but no two are ever the same. I'm still discovering mine."

"Just how are you going to train me?" Selene asked her.

Mia set her empty plate down and wiped her hands on her jeans as she stood up. "Like this," she said, and before Selene could argue, Mia reached down and gripped Selene's wrists and yanked her to her feet. One moment they were standing on the back deck; the next, they stood in a vast dessert.

The extra layer of her sweatshirt made her instantly sticky and sweaty.

"What..." Selene blinked a few times, then glanced around. All around them, in the far distance, there were tall mountains. From this far, she couldn't see anything beyond their massive gray shapes. Then Selene glanced up into the sky. "There are three suns." She pointed to the sky.

Mia smiled as she stood beside her, watching her face. "Yes, and six moons at night."

"This is..." She tried to remember what Mia had called it. "Your Void?"

Mia nodded. "It's actually another world. I've tried to chart the stars, but..." She shrugged. "It's basically impossible."

"You're saying we're standing on another planet?" Selene glanced around, suddenly worried about alien life coming after them.

Mia chuckled. "It's void of life. Hence the name," she said, as if reading Selene's mind.

"Nothing lives here?"

Mia's eyes darkened slightly as she shook her head. "Once, but not now."

Selene took a relaxing breath. "Okay, so, how did you bring me here?"

"The art of surprise." Mia smiled. "You may not have been able to bring Scott into your Beyond because he has never wanted to go."

Selene frowned. "You're saying that I haven't been able to take him there not because of me, but because of him?"

Mia nodded. "It's worth a try. When we return, I'll suggest you try taking him to your Beyond. To test the theory. If I'm right, it shouldn't work. But then you can try again when he's not expecting it."

"Why couldn't you have told me all this in the city?" Selene asked.

Mia's eyes closed for a moment. When they opened again, they locked with her own. "We're supposed to be here. Something is coming for you. For Scott. He is more dangerous than you know."

Selene felt a shiver race through her.

CHAPTER TEN

Scott watched Mia and Selene disappear and jumped to his feet. Before he could cry out, however, they were back, standing before him.

"What the..." He gripped Selene. "Are you okay?"

Selene smiled at him and nodded. "Yes, I'm fine. Mia just took me to her Void place. It's quite hot and beautiful."

Mia nodded as she sat down. "Why don't you try to take Scott to your Beyond place?"

Selene swallowed as she turned to him and held out her hand. "Shall we give it a try?"

Scott took a deep breath and took her hand. As with each time she'd tried in the past, nothing happened.

Selene turned to Mia who smiled. "Told you."

Then Selene surprised him by leaning up on her toes and kissing him. It wasn't just a simple peck on the lips either. Her body pressed against his, her lips melted to him. Her taste surrounded him, and he lost all thoughts in his head except enjoying the feel and taste of her.

When she pulled back, he was so consumed with what the kiss had done to him, that it didn't register at first. But then he realized he couldn't see her face clearly. He blinked a couple of times.

Had it been this dark before?

Selene gasped and then her smile doubled. "I did it," she said, clapping and bouncing up and down slightly.

"Did what?" He finally looked around. "What the hell?" he asked, tensing.

Instead of standing on the back deck, they were standing under a dark sky. Everywhere around them were dull colors instead of the vibrant greens and yellows of the fields that had surrounded the farmhouse. Even the air smelled different.

It wasn't cold, but a shiver ran through him the moment he realized where he was.

"This is the Beyond," he said under his breath.

"Yes." Selene smiled up at him.

"How? I thought you'd tried." He frowned.

"It was Mia's idea. She suggested that the reason I've never been able to bring you here isn't because of me." She paused. "It's because of you. Because you were resisting it."

He took a deep breath and glanced around. Outside of the odd colors, strange smell, and the feeling of unease, he would have assumed he was on Earth on a winter evening walk. "It's strange."

"Yes. You should see the rivers of fire." She took his hand and tried to tug him.

"I... maybe we can save that for our second trip?" he suggested, wanting to get back. "I don't want to freak Mia out."

"Time moves differently here," she said easily. "Mia and I were in the Void for almost half an hour. But it was probably just a blink of an eye for you."

"It was seconds," he agreed. "So time moves faster here?"

She shrugged. "Something like that." Her hand was in his and she tugged slightly. "The river is just up here."

He frowned. "Do you always appear in the same place?" he asked as he followed her down a worn pathway.

"Yes," she answered over her shoulder.

"How far have you explored?" he asked as he ducked under a branch.

"Very far." She smiled at him. "Here." She stopped and lifted a branch full of dull brown leaves.

Just beyond was a large river and, as she had explained, it was made of what looked like red glowing lava.

"It's not hot," she said, moving closer. "You'd think it was lava, but it's not, it's water. The best I can explain is that color is wrong here." She motioned to the sky.

For the first time, he looked up. Really looked. He'd believed the sky was dark, like the night sky, but it was actually a dull gold color. There were no stars, no moon, nothing other than a shimmer of gold above them.

"It appears closer than it is." She looked up. "Come on." She took his hand again.

He followed her through the trees and along the banks of the lava river. Since he felt no heat coming off the red stream, he relaxed as they made their way up a hill.

"This is my favorite view," she said, eagerly.

Once they reached the crest, she stopped and motioned below them.

It was as if they had climbed a very tall mountain. The view below them was so vast that he couldn't distinguish where the land disappeared. There were many rivers of fire below them that all filled into one larger river that flowed away from them to the right. He could just make out small hills and valleys as he scanned the horizon.

"Does anyone live here?" he asked her after figuring out why he found the landscape odd. There weren't any houses or roads.

"Not that I've seen. I used to be afraid when I was younger. I'd imagine all sorts of creatures hiding, ready to jump out and gobble up a small girl like me." She laughed. "But then I realized there wasn't so much as a mouse or bug." She motioned around her.

He frowned as he turned to her. "Your brother wants me here to wake up the devil? Does that mean, somewhere, out there"—he waved his hand over the view—"he's sleeping now?"

Selene frowned and shivered. Instead of answering, she took his hand and as fast as they had arrived, they were back, standing on the deck with Mia, who was sitting in the exact same place she had been when they'd left.

"It worked." Mia smiled.

Selene sat down and sighed as she rubbed her hands up and down her arms as if to get warm.

"Did something happen?" Mia asked when he sat down and remained quiet too.

"No." Selene shook her head. "I guess I'm just tired from the long day. I might take a nap." She stood up. "Thanks for this," she said to Mia.

Mia nodded.

"I'm going to let you rest," Scott said as he lifted his soda and took a sip.

When they were alone, he turned to Mia. "She's afraid," he said clearly.

"Yes." Mia nodded. "If she's going to survive what comes next, she'll need to get over that fear."

"How does she do that?"

Mia ran her eyes over him. "You're her strength."

"I am?" He almost laughed. Then he realized it was true. So true, his chest started to ache.

Mia's smile grew. "I knew there was something special about you when I first saw you move into the building."

His eyes narrowed. "What exactly do you do for a living that you can afford to take off?"

She laughed. "This is it." She motioned around. "Djinn don't need jobs."

He shook his head. "Why live in the city then?"

"Okay, so I do have a job. I actually work at the coffee shop as a barista, but it's not really..." She shook her head. "My real job is to help people. I'm like a lightning rod. People who need my help the most are drawn to me. Which is why it pays to work in a public place. Normally, I can spot them as soon as they walk in. I've been keeping my eye on you for a while. Then, when Selene showed up, I knew why you were special."

He frowned at this bit of information. No man wanted to hear that they were only special because of someone else. Still, hadn't he always felt that around Selene?

He knew other people saw her as strange. She normally wore all black, kept to herself, and never got close to anyone other than him. If he hadn't known her, he would have thought her strange too.

But to him, Selene was... well, just Selene. Someone he couldn't imagine life without.

"I have some lessons for you as well," Mia said, shifting. "Hold out your hands." She held her hands out.

After a moment, he shifted and set his hands in hers, palms up.

The moment his eyes met Mia's, the entire world

seemed to tilt and then shift. He felt as if he was on the Tilt-A-Whirl, one of those old carnival rides he and Selene had snuck onto as kids.

He must have groaned because Mia shushed him.

"It'll pass," she said softly.

He closed his eyes, feeling the sandwich he'd just eaten threaten to come back up.

Then, the swirling stopped. He opened his eyes and realized that everything had stopped.

"This is the Between. It's a safe place." Mia dropped his hands and stood up. "We can practice here."

"Practice?" he asked, standing up. Everything was stopped as he suspected. There was a bird hovering in the air about a hundred feet off the ground, not far from them. Its wings were stretched out, as if it was using them to glide, but it wasn't moving.

"Sure." Mia motioned to him. He followed her down to the grassy yard. He glanced back at the house, worried about Selene.

"She's safe. She won't even know we're gone." Mia motioned to him. "Show me what you've got."

He frowned. "Like?"

"Fight me." She moved, positioning her feet shoulder-width apart.

He laughed. "I am not going to fight you."

"Why not? Afraid?" she challenged with a smile.

He laughed again. "First off, I'm probably a hundred pounds heavier and a foot taller than you."

"So, you are afraid." She wiggled her finger. "I'll go easy on you."

He shook his head. "Nope, not going to." He crossed his arms over his chest. He remembered trying the same thing with Selene when they were teenagers. He'd ended up in the ER with a broken wrist for the trouble.

He didn't know if Mia had super strength like Selene did, but he wasn't going to chance it.

"I'll dare you that you won't even lay a finger on me," Mia said with a tilt of her head.

"Dare?" He laughed. "What are we twelve?"

"Okay, a wager then. Loser cooks dinner." Then she added, "For the duration of our stay."

He chuckled. "I don't want to hurt you."

Mia lifted her chin in challenge. "Try it. I promise, in the Between, no one can get hurt."

He frowned. "No one?"

She stood straight and glanced around. Then she lifted a large chunk of firewood and chucked it at his head. He didn't even have time to duck. The thing hit him square in the face and bounced off as if it were made of rubber. He hadn't even felt it.

"Okay. Game changer," he said, raising his fists.

What seemed like half an hour later, he was covered in sweat and had yet to even put a finger on Mia.

"It seems sort of unfair now that I know you have a black belt in pretty much every martial art," he said, as they headed back up the stairs to the deck.

"You really need to work on your self-defense. I'd suggest taking some classes yourself," Mia added. "How are you supposed to defend yourself against what's coming?"

"What *is* coming?" he asked, suddenly worried.

"Only Selene can answer that," she replied. "For now, I'm going to enjoy having you cook all week." She stopped at the top of the stairs and looked at him, her eyes narrowing slightly. "You can cook, right?"

He nodded. "Yeah, it's one of the things I can do very well."

"Good," she said when they stood where they had. "Brace yourself. Sometimes people don't adjust well when things start moving again."

The next moment, he was thrust back into the seat he was standing in front of, as if some invisible force had pushed him.

"What was that?" he asked with a frown.

"That," she said as she took up her glass of wine and took a sip, "was your body feeling the Earth starting to rotate again." She smiled.

CHAPTER ELEVEN

When Selene woke from her short nap, Scott and Mia were in the kitchen, laughing as if they were old friends. Scott was stirring something at the stove, and Selene realized she was starving.

"Did you have a good nap?" Mia asked her.

"Yes, I suppose it was the car trip." She shrugged, feeling stupid for needing a nap in the middle of the day. But the truth was, she'd been exhausted after the trip to the Beyond. She supposed it was because she'd brought Scott along, but in truth, she was also tired because she'd been up most of the night with Scott. Plus, she'd needed some time to herself to think about what her brother had told her the last time they'd spoken.

She wondered if he was still in New York. Or if he had really been there.

"What have the two of you been up to?" she asked, sitting beside Mia.

"Training," Mia said. "Scott needs it just as bad as you do."

"Training?" she asked with a frown.

"Mia has this place..."

"The Between," Mia supplied.

"Yeah." Scott nodded as he flipped what appeared like chicken in the pan. "Time stops and nothing can hurt you. So I tried to kick her butt and didn't even touch her. Which is why I'm cooking dinner every night we're here," he added with a smile.

"Okay." Selene tried to process everything Scott had just said.

"Mia is a black belt in judo, jujutsu, tae kwon do, and kick boxing," Scott said without glancing back.

Selene looked at the small woman with a newfound appreciation.

"Not all of us are indestructible like you," Mia shrugged. "It's all part of the djinn training."

"What else?" Selene walked over and poured herself a glass of wine from a bottle that was sitting on the countertop.

"Training?" Mia asked with a sigh. When Selene nodded, she continued. "All the basics. Weapons training, self-defense, driving, you name it. Anything my parents thought I needed to protect myself and the future."

Selene had never thought of training herself. She'd been picked on plenty as a kid, but whenever a bully went to hit her, they'd pull away quicky enough and run in the opposite direction, never to come near her again. Besides, with her strength and the ability to never be hurt, she doubted she needed any training. But Scott...

He turned off the stove and turned towards her. Suddenly, images of him being hurt flooded her mind, memories of every time he'd been injured over the years.

The time he'd broken his wrist in basketball. When he'd

twisted his ankle or taken a ball to the face and almost broken his perfect nose.

Her stomach lurched and she felt sick thinking of him getting hurt because she'd brought him along on the journey.

This was a very bad idea. He should go back home. Tonight.

She was quiet as they ate dinner. Mia and Scott acted more like brother and sister than they did. It was fun to see and even with the heaviness looming over her mind, she ended up laughing a few times.

After dinner, she and Mia did the dishes while Scott carried a few pieces of firewood in and started a fire in the fireplace.

They decided to watch a movie together, and Mia made a huge bowl of popcorn with extra butter on it.

After the movie, they all headed off to their rooms.

"Spill," Scott said the moment they were alone.

She groaned loudly and plopped down on the edge of the bed. "It's annoying that you know me so well."

He crossed his arms over his chest and narrowed his eyes at her. "You aren't jealous of Mia, are you?"

"What?" Selene frowned. "No. Of course not."

Scott relaxed. "Good, because I like her like a sister."

"Yeah, that's obvious." She fell backwards onto the bed and stared up at the ceiling.

Scott moved over and sat on the bed, looking down at her. "So what's been eating you since you woke up from your nap? You didn't get another visit from your brother, did you?"

"No," she said, turning towards him.

He lifted her head and placed it in his lap and started

running his fingers through her hair, something he knew she really enjoyed.

"You should go home," she blurted out, closing her eyes.

His fingers stilled, tangled in her hair. "Why should I?"

She opened her eyes now and looked deep within his eyes. "Because you could get hurt."

He smiled and then leaned down and brushed his lips against hers. "I could get hurt at home too."

"Not like...this." How could she tell him that his life was in far more danger being around her then it was sitting behind some desk in an office?

"Selene." He cupped her face and shifted until he was lying beside her. He wrapped his arms around her body, holding her tight. "I'm not going anywhere." He kissed her again.

She knew it was a futile effort to try and get him to go. Over the years, she'd never really been able to change his mind on anything.

"Then we're just going to have to step up your training," she said against his jaw as she wrapped her legs around his hips and spun until she was hovering over him.

He was laughing as she gripped his wrists and held them over his head.

"Do you really believe I would fight you right now?" he said in a low tone as she felt his excitement grow against her core.

She moved her hips and stroked him a few times as she leaned down and covered his mouth with hers.

"I don't think you could even if you wanted to." She smiled as she lifted his shirt over his head, then ran her lips and her fingers over his chest. She unsnapped his jeans and pulled them down his hips, along with his boxer shorts. When she cupped him, she glanced up at him and waited until his eyes locked with hers. "Besides, we both know I always win," she purred, and then she took him into her mouth.

His fingers dug into her hair and a low groan filled the room. The sexy noises were building up her own needs, and she yanked off her own pants and shirt.

Before she could remove her bra and panties, however, he was flipping her under him.

"Let me enjoy these for a moment." He ran a finger over the silk and lace she was wearing. Normally, she only had on a sports bra and boy shorts, but for him, she'd pulled out her good underwear. "Nice," he said as his finger circled her nipples through the thin material.

"You're killing me." She groaned.

"Good," he said with a slight chuckle.

She was the one moaning when he slipped a finger under the edge of her panties and ran it across her. Her hips jerked without her thinking.

She was still new to this sex-with-a-partner thing, but she was pretty sure he was doing something to her that most men couldn't.

"Scott," she said, pulling his mouth back down to hers. "Please."

She felt his smile next to her lips before he quickly disappeared. When he returned, he pulled off her panties and bra and slid on a condom.

"I could get used to this," she said, running her fingers over his chest.

"Me too." He leaned in, kissed her, and slid deep inside her. "Home," he said softly next to her lips, and her heart melted.

Selene lay in the dark room, mentally kicking herself for allowing herself to believe, even for a moment, that there could be any kind of future for them. She knew better.

After almost an hour of not being able to sleep, she got up quietly, pulled on Scott's T-shirt, and tiptoed out onto the patio. It was cool, and she wished immediately that she'd thought to put on some pants.

The moment she thought it, fire burst from her fingertips, and she squealed loudly and shook her hands vigorously to put out the fire.

"What?" Scott was there, by her side, still completely naked.

"I..." She looked down at her fingertips. The fire was gone. She thought about the cold and wishing to be warm and—boom!—the fire was back.

"What the..." Scott took a step back. Not from fear, but because he hadn't wanted to get burned. "Seriously?" he asked with a chuckle.

"I was cold." She frowned as she waved her fingers, and the fire was gone.

"I'm going back to bed." Scott turned and disappeared into the room again, shutting the door behind him.

She supposed that, after growing up around her, there was little that he would be surprised at anymore.

She smiled and lit the fires again and waved her fingers in the darkness.

"Having fun?" Lucas asked as he leaned against the brick post a few feet away from her.

Selene flicked out the fire, feeling very warm all over thanks to the newfound power.

"What do you want?" she asked, annoyed that he would be there, in her mind, at a time like this.

"The same thing as last time," he answered, glancing

towards the doors where Scott had just disappeared. "You know how to do it now."

"No." She shook her head, whispering since she didn't want to alarm Scott that her brother had invaded her mind once again.

"It's inevitable," he said, straightening up.

"Why? Why him?" She crossed her arms over her chest.

"He's more powerful than you know," Lucas said with a slight frown. "He just hasn't awoken yet."

"What does that mean?" She shook her head.

"It means we have a lot of work to do." Lucas took another step towards her. "Why don't you let me in so we can get started?"

Selene frowned and suddenly it dawned on her. In the past, when Lucas had visited her, they were always somewhere else. Dressed different. Now, however, they were still standing on the back patio, and she was still just wearing her boy short underwear under Scott's oversized T-shirt.

"You..." She walked over and pushed her hand against Lucas's shoulder. The man was solid and really standing in front of her. "You're here." She felt her heart leap as fear consumed her.

CHAPTER TWELVE

"What do you want?" Scott asked Lucas when the four of them sat in the kitchen as the sun rose slowly outside. Mia was making coffee. Selene was sitting at the end of the bar looking tired and grumpy.

Helios, or rather Lucas, was nothing like he'd imagined. Instead of a dark sinister-looking villain, the man was good-looking enough to be a model. He dressed in very expensive clothing and had his jet-black hair cut short around the sides and longer on top.

It was his eyes that stood out though. Their eerie gold color left an impression in Scott's mind.

"As I've mentioned to Selene, I'm in need of your assistance," Lucas said, his eyes moving to Mia. "What exactly are you?" he asked, nodding towards her.

Mia smiled. "Your worst nightmare if you cause problems."

For the first time since Selene had shown her brother in, Lucas smiled.

"Interesting." Lucas turned back to him. "You need to awaken your powers."

"You said we had until the next full moon. Why are you here now?" Selene asked Lucas.

"To help him awaken his powers." Lucas looked at Scott.

"What powers?" Scott shook his head, then turned to Selene. "Like Selene has?"

"No," Lucas said firmly. "You are... more."

"Which means?" he asked, feeling a pit in his stomach.

As an answer, Lucas stood up from the barstool and turned into a large black wolf dog. It was so massive, its fur nearly touched the ceiling.

"Mia can do that too," Selene said, and the wolf/dog's yellow eyes turned to Mia, who nodded.

"Show me," Lucas, or rather the dog, said firmly.

Mia set down the mug of coffee she was holding and shifted before their eyes.

They both stared at one another for a moment before turning back into themselves.

"Don't your clothes get ripped off?" Scott asked, suddenly feeling stupid when he realized he'd asked that question out loud. He cleared his throat. "I mean, you just shifted into furry dogs."

"Hellhounds," Lucas corrected.

"Seriously?" Mia asked. "I've always thought of myself more as a dog."

The corner of Lucas lips curved up almost into a smile.

"It takes three of us," Lucas said. "Now I know who the third is." He nodded to Mia.

"So, I am needed." She smiled as she picked up the mug and then walked over and handed it to Selene.

"And Selene is our ticket to hell," Lucas said, taking the other mug of coffee from Selene.

"So, what? I'm just supposed to deliver the three of you

to the Beyond," she said firmly, "and watch you wake up the devil?"

"Not the devil. In sense. I mean..." Lucas actually looked irritated or... embarrassed. "Yes, his name is Hades, but no, he's not the devil in Western mythology or religion. Think of him as... the gatekeeper to the destruction of everything."

"Then why wake him?" Scott asked.

"Because there is a rip in the gates. A leak. One that only he can mend," Lucas explained.

"Okay, so..." Mia leaned on the counter. "Hades is a good guy?"

"Yes and no. Once we wake him, we will need to get out of there quickly. Selene will deliver us three, we will wake him, then change into..." He motioned with his hands.

"Hellhounds," Mia supplied.

Lucas nodded. "And let Hades find and fix the leak."

"How do you know there's a leak?" Selene asked.

Lucas eyes moved to her. "Because that is how our parents escaped."

Selene frowned. "Right."

He jerked his head around. "If you knew about that, knew about the dangers Selene and Tara were in, why didn't you help them?"

"Because I was not meant to," Lucas answered. His eyes moved to Mia. "I am, however, meant to be here."

"Okay, so how do we train Scott to ..."—Mia waved her hand in front of her—"change?"

"Why can Scott change?" Selene interrupted. "I mean, Mia is... what she is. You are the son of... who you are. Scott is nothing. I mean..." Selene touched his arm. "His parents..."

"Were just as important as ours were. Most sons and

daughters of gods are not raised in happy households. We're abandoned at birth. Left to be raised by any caring soul who stumbles upon us. I was adopted by Leif and Leslie Romano."

"And your name? Helios?" Scott asked.

"I came with it." He took a sip of his coffee. "Much like my sisters. But when I was adopted, my parents called me Lucas instead."

"Okay, so if Scott's parents were gods, which ones?" Selene asked him.

Lucas's eyes bore into his. "I cannot tell you. Only a..." Lucas frowned and turned back to Mia and then smiled as if he suddenly got a joke. "Only a djinn can."

Mia smiled. "Figured me out, huh?"

Lucas nodded as if in appreciation. "I have never met one of your kind before. It took me a moment."

"There's currently only one of me on this planet," Mia answered with a grin.

Lucas nodded. "It is a pleasure meeting you."

"So, how do we train Scott to do what we can do?" Mia asked.

"Much like you train a dog to sit," Lucas said. "With a lot of help and patience."

"Don't forget the treats. I'm starving," Scott said, earning a few chuckles.

"Okay then. How about we start training after breakfast?" Mia asked.

Almost two hours later, after everyone was fed, showered, and dressed for the day, the four of them stood in the tall grass behind the house.

Since Scott had been to Mia's Between before, he stood and watched the others take it all in. Mia explained how no one could get hurt by tossing a log at each of their heads, much like she'd done to him. Only, Lucas changed into the dog form quickly and caught the massive log in his mouth, like a dog would catch a stick.

"I think he likes it," Mia joked. "We can play fetch later." She winked at Lucas, who quickly changed back into human form and tossed the log to the side, looking slightly annoyed at Mia.

"Shall we begin?" Lucas turned to Scott. "The first thing you need to realize is…"

Scott tuned out. He had no clue how he was going to turn himself into a dog or even if he really could. His entire life there had been nothing special about him. Selene held all the awards in that field.

He glanced over at her and realized she was watching him with a worried look in her eyes. He reached over and took her hand and squeezed it to reassure her.

Lucas was still talking to him, but he wasn't paying attention.

"Hey." Lucas snapped his fingers in front of Scott's face then glared over at Selene. "You're distracting him."

Selene dropped his hand and stepped back. "We'll go over here and spar," Mia told Selene. "It will be interesting to fight someone as strong as you."

The two of them moved away, and Scott turned his attention to Lucas again.

"Put your feelings aside," Lucas warned as his eyes narrowed.

Scott wanted to tell the guy it was easy for him because, obviously, the man had never had any feelings, outside of anger and annoyance.

"Right." Scott nodded and focused on the task at hand. "So, you really expect me to just"—he snapped his fingers—"change into a dog?"

"Hellhound," Lucas corrected.

"Not going to call it that," Scott said with a shake of his head.

He thought he saw Lucas' lips curve slightly into a smile.

"Yes," he answered.

"When did you turn the first time? How did you know you could?" Scott asked.

"I was five," Lucas answered with a frown. "I didn't know I could until I had."

Scott figured there was more to the story but shrugged and waved his hands. "Okay, walk me through it."

For the next hour, he listened to Selene's brother explain how to change. What his mind needed to be focused on, how his body should feel when it started to change, and most importantly, how to breathe through it all.

Nothing seemed to work, and Lucas grew annoyed at him.

Finally, Mia interrupted them and suggested they break for lunch.

He was thankful and spent his entire lunch break talking quietly with Selene on the back deck while Mia disappeared into her room and Lucas went off somewhere on his own to make a few phone calls.

"What is it that your brother does for a living?" he asked Selene.

"You know, I don't know." She chuckled. "He must make a lot of money. His clothes are expensive, and did you see the car in the driveway?" She shook her head. "Way out of our price range."

"What do you know about him?" he asked, suddenly worried. It was obvious by the man's appearance and abilities that he was Selene's brother. The two of them looked more alike than Tara and Selene did. Still, he could see some resemblance between the sisters.

"He lives in New York. Was adopted, but I'm not sure how old he was when he was finally taken in." Selene frowned. "That's about it."

Just then Mia stepped out on the deck with an iced tea in her hand.

"I can tell you more about him," Mia said, sitting down across from them.

"You can?" Selene frowned. "How do you know?"

Mia sighed and then shifted until her legs were tucked underneath her. She set the glass down and closed her eyes.

"He's the oldest of the three of you," she began. "He has an apartment in New York and goes there often for business but lives in upstate New York. He works for..."—she frowned—"his father's company. I... can't see what..."

"What are you doing?" Lucas' voice broke in, causing the three of them to jump slightly.

"We were curious about you," Selene said, unapologetic. "Since you seem determined not to tell us more, Mia was helping us out." She waved her hand towards Mia, who was sipping her tea and avoiding looking at Lucas.

"You could have asked," Lucas said, sitting down. His eyes bore into Mia's.

"Would you have answered?" Selene asked.

Lucas turned to her. "No," he said firmly.

"I thought not. Which is why I was allowing Mia to fill us in," Selene said with a nod of her head.

"We have to know we can trust you," Scott added.

Lucas turned his gaze towards him. "You work for Forge International."

Scott tensed. "Yes, how do— "

"My family owns the company," Lucas said. "I'm the CEO."

Scott was quiet for a moment. "Did you know I worked there before you contacted your sister?"

"My sister is the reason you work there," Lucas said, confirming Scott's new suspicions.

It was obvious now. In the last year, he'd been offered a high-paying job with the firm. He had quickly left his old job with a smaller firm without so much as a glance back.

Thanks to the position, he'd been able to get his apartment and even his car.

"How long have you known about me? Before you contacted me last week?" Selene asked.

Scott glanced over at her, and he could see the hurt in her eyes.

Lucas seemed to soften. "For years."

"Why did you wait until now to contact me? Have you even talked to Tara?" Selene crossed her arms over her chest.

"No," he answered. "I waited until the time was right. I haven't reached out to Tara. Yet. When this is all over, I hope we can... become close."

Selene suddenly stood up and headed towards the stairs. He moved to follow her, but Lucas put a hand on his shoulder. "No, this is for me." He followed Selene down the stairs.

"He's not wrong you know," Mia said once they were alone.

"About?" he asked.

"If he had contacted her before now, the timeline would be off. The chances of us beating what is coming would have narrowed." She turned towards him. "This was our only path. Our one shot."

CHAPTER THIRTEEN

Selene needed some time alone. The anger about the missed years she could have known she had family out there boiled so deep inside her that, the moment her feet touched the soft grass, she shot up into the air, not giving a damn who might see her. What could her life had been like if Lucas had reached out to her years ago? Would she and Scott have suffered as much as they had growing up?

Lucas' family, the one that had taken him in, had money. She and Scott had none growing up. They had nothing. Only each other.

Would they have grown as close as they had if Lucas had come into her life before? In her heart, she knew the answer and released most of the frustration and hurt.

She had needed the cold air on her face, the clouds beneath her, to think clearly and release the anger from her heart. She had just started relaxing when a voice from behind her had her screaming.

"Sorry," Lucas apologized.

The fact that her brother was flying beside her had her anger growing.

"Why didn't you tell us you could fly?" she barked out as she hovered in mid-air.

"Again, no one asked." He shrugged, crossing his arms over his chest. On the ground, it would have looked intimidating, but with the ground more than a mile below them, it was almost comical. "What?" He frowned at her.

She couldn't help it. At that moment, she burst out laughing. Uncontrollably. She even hugged her sides as her laughter echoed in the clouds.

What felt like ten minutes later, she finally settled down. Her sides hurt and there were tears streaming down her cheeks.

"Feel better?" Lucas asked with a grin on his face.

"You can smile." She pointed to his face.

"I can do a lot of things. Which I would have gladly told anyone who asked," he retorted.

"Okay, I'm asking now. What else can you do?" She crossed her arms over her chest.

He glanced around. The clouds had cleared a little, so that they could clearly see they were alone and far too high for anyone to see them.

He lifted his hand, and a fireball shot from his fingertips and sailed across the sky, fizzling out about a hundred yards from them.

She smiled and lifted her hand and had a ball of flames following the same path.

"Not bad." He nodded. "Okay, how about this one." His smile grew as he disappeared before her eyes.

"Invisible?" She gasped. "I've got to try that." She narrowed her eyes and focused. She was focusing so hard that when her hand disappeared in front of her, she almost didn't notice.

"Not bad," Lucas said, reappearing.

She relaxed her mind and noticed that her hand reappeared.

"The next bit we should be on the ground for," he suggested.

The trip to the skies had done what she'd wanted. Her mind was clear of the anger, but there were still answers she needed.

"Why did you wait until now?" she asked him.

Thankfully, her brother didn't play dumb and answered.

"It wasn't time. There is an order to things. Like when playing chess, you have to move your pieces around before you strike. If we're going to win the next battle"—he glanced downwards to where the ranch sat directly below them—"we have to follow the pattern set before us. We can only move our pieces in certain directions."

She followed his gaze below. "Scott?" she asked.

"And Mia." He frowned, then looked back up at her. "I know she may not think it, but she is just as important as the rest of us. I could not have approached her myself. I needed her to meet you, first. To do that, I had to place Scott in her building."

Selene narrowed her eyes. "All this"—she waved her hands—"was to get to Mia?"

Lucas sighed. "In a way. She is... a very important piece. There are two others that we will need, but not for this battle. Not until..." He shook his head. "I'm getting ahead of myself. Let's go down. It's chilly up here and your friends are worried." He motioned to below them.

Sure enough, she could see two small dots standing in the middle of the grassy yard now.

"One last question," she said.

"Sure." Lucas motioned for her to continue.

"How long did you know about Tara and me? Who you were? Who we were?" she asked.

"That's three questions," he said with a slight smile. "I was in the same field you were when Tara arrived."

Selene frowned. "You were there? I... didn't I see you?"

"Our sixteenth birthday. I had come into some of my powers, but after that night, everything became clearer. One of my powers is sight. Of sorts. Like Tara and you. Only... I can see multiple moves ahead. Possibilities. Outcomes if we chose the wrong path."

"And this is our best possibility?" she asked as they started their descent.

"Yes," Lucas said as their feet touched the ground a yard from Mia and Scott. "This is it." Lucas' eyes were on them. "It's up to us."

She didn't want to tell him that she felt a little left out. After all, she and Tara had been left out of the last fight.

What good were her powers if not to fight? Her strength, her inability to be hurt, and even her flight and now invisibility—surely she had them for some greater purpose.

Was she just a taxi service to the Beyond?

For the rest of that day and the next few that followed, Scott worked with Lucas. The four of them grew more relaxed around one another. Mia even seemed to be warming up to Lucas, including him in her jokes.

If it wasn't for Mia's humor and good nature, the time would have gone by a lot slower than it did. Passing her nights in Scott's arms didn't hurt either.

Since Scott had yet to transform into a dog, Lucas suggested they remain on the ranch to continue the work. Since he was technically Scott's boss and could easily arrange for his time away, they all agreed.

"I told them you're working on a special project for me," Lucas said, "which is technically true."

Each day, they worked out in the yard, rain or shine. Most days it was cool. Halloween came and went, and still they worked.

They used the hot tub most nights since she and Mia spent most of their days sparring.

Lucas decided it would help settle Scott's mind if they too trained most of the day. They worked on getting Scott into the right mind to transform. But the more time that passed, the more frustrated Scott grew and the surer he became that Lucas had the wrong guy.

Then one day, before they stepped outside, Lucas asked her to join them instead of going off with Mia.

"Go with me on this," Lucas whispered to her as they stepped outside.

The moment they stood in the middle of the yard, Lucas nodded to Mia.

Then, without warning, a dark shadowy figure appeared between her and Lucas and grabbed them. Her arm was yanked behind her back, and she and Lucas disappeared with a scream.

The moment they vanished, Lucas rushed to her and clasped his hand over her mouth. Somehow, Mia had caused the smoke figure to appear while Lucas had turned them invisible.

The pair of them stood feet from Scott and watched the sheer panic flood Scott's face.

"What the—!" Scott growled, as he scanned the yard. Then, as they watched, Scott's body shivered and grew larger. The low growl echoed through the yard as Mia watched on.

Scott looked so desperate. So scared. Selene wanted to go to him, to push Lucas away and reappear.

She didn't know why, but in all that time, she hadn't told Scott about her new ability to vanish. Maybe she'd just forgotten? Maybe it was one more thing she didn't want him to worry about?

Either way, she desperately wished she had told him now.

He shivered again and they watched long dark hairs grow on his arms, which were growing longer and contorting. His hands turned to paws. His nose grew longer, and so did his ears.

It took no more than a minute, and she held her breath the entire time, Lucas's hand still over her mouth.

When the transformation was complete, Scott lunged forward, missing them by no more than a foot.

Lucas quickly released her and reappeared as he transformed.

She watched in horror as the two large animals stood across from one another and growled as they circled the yard.

"Easy!" Mia yelled. "You've made your point," she said to Lucas.

Then it dawned on Selene. Mia had yet to take them to the safety of the Between. They were still in the real world. Where someone could get hurt.

Taking a chance, she raised her hands and stepped between the two of them. Their shoulders were easily taller than her head.

"Enough!" she screamed through the loud growls.

Lucas's yellow eyes narrowed slightly before he turned back into himself. Scott stopped growling and, after running his eyes over her to make sure she was okay, he relaxed and turned back.

"Holy hell," Scott said with a sigh as he rushed over to her and wrapped his arms around her. "I thought... What happened? Where did you go?"

She winced. "Mia made that smoke creature, and we can... sort of... become invisible."

Scott jerked back and looked down at her. "Seriously?" The look in his eyes wasn't one of anger or hurt that she hadn't told him. Instead, he seemed... impressed. "That is so cool."

She laughed. "Are we going to talk about you changing into a dog?"

He frowned. "I did?"

She nodded. "Yeah."

He glanced around and everyone nodded.

"I don't know why I didn't try this earlier," Lucas said proudly.

"It was my idea," Mia added, crossing her arms over her chest.

"Right." Lucas basically ignored her. "Shall we try that again?" he asked Scott.

"The kidnapping part?" Scott frowned.

"I think now that you have done it once, you'll be able to repeat your actions. Just go back to what you were thinking, feeling, and do it again." He waved his hand.

Selene took a few steps away from Scott and waited.

Scott's eyes turned to her and there was no hiding the love in them. One minute he was standing in front of her, the next, he was a large black dog.

She smiled as she walked over and pet him between the ears when he lowered his head towards her.

"I've always wanted a pet," she joked, and he licked her

face, leaving a stream of salvia over her face and soaking the front of her hair. "Eww!" She jerked back and wiped her face with her shirt.

Scott reappeared in front of her, laughing. "You deserved that for tricking me."

"This calls for a celebration," Mia pointed out, and she started heading back to the house.

At that moment, the entire ground shifted. It was as if a huge earthquake was hitting the yard. The house in the distance didn't shake, only the four of them, in the yard.

"It is almost time." A deep voice echoed in each of their minds, followed by a high-pitched screeching that had everyone doubling over in pain. "You cannot stop me," the voice hissed. "I am your doom. Your destiny. Your destruction."

Then, just as quickly as the shaking had started, it stopped, leaving the four of them shaken and a little unsteady in the empty yard.

"Do you want to tell us what the hell that was?" Scott turned to Lucas.

"That was your father," Lucas answered with a frown. "We're going to need that drink first," he said, and marched towards the house.

CHAPTER FOURTEEN

S cott downed the second shot of bourbon that Lucas handed him as he waited for Mia and Selene to pour them all glasses of wine.

"Maybe we can start a fire," Mia suggested. "It's cold."

"I'll do it." Lucas walked over to the fireplace. Instead of bending down and lighting a match, he opened his palm and a ball of fire shot out from his fingertips.

"Great," Scott groaned. "Now he shoots fire from his fingers." Then he remembered Selene doing something similar and sunk down on the sofa.

Mia handed him a glass of wine, and he downed almost half of it as Selene sat next to him.

"Are you okay?" Selene asked quietly.

"Sure," he replied, already feeling the bourbon and the wine loosen his tension.

Lucas took his glass and sat next to Mia.

Everyone watched him and waited.

"Have you heard of Moros?" Lucas asked.

"No," everyone said together.

"He's basically the god of doom," Lucas answered.

"Great, and he's my father?" Scott asked. "No wonder my life has been shit."

Selene took his hand, and he realized that statement wasn't completely true. She'd been there with him through it all.

"I had my suspicions. It's the reason you're meant to help stop him," Lucas said.

"So, the god of doom and the devil are supposed to fight?" Mia asked.

"No, the legends say that Prometheus saved mankind from Moros with the gift of hope in the form of the goddess Elpis. Elpis is the essence of hope. However, some legends are wrong. The one where Moros overpowers Elpis, his sister, and locks her away in Pandora's box, whose location can only to be revealed by the three Fates. She isn't really locked in a box somewhere. Instead, Pandora will unleash Elpis somehow, so she can fight her brother."

Selene got a shiver down her spin and leaned into Scott, who wrapped his arm around her.

"The three Fates?" Scott asked.

"Clotho, Lachesis, and Atropos. The three that are one who spin the thread of human fates. At death, they cut the life threads."

"Where are they?" Selene asked.

"Where does Mia come into all this?" Scott asked. "I mean, I get it, she can turn into a..."

"Hellhound?" Lucas added.

"Dog," Scott countered, and Selene watched her brother's lips curve. She now understood that this was his smile, or the only hint of one that he had.

"She is more complicated." Lucas turned to Mia.

"As a djinn, it's my life's work to help those in need," she said firmly.

Lucas made a noise and then cleared his throat. "For now, we'll just be thankful she is here." He turned to Selene, and she understood. It's what their parents had said. What everyone in Hidden Creek understood. She and Scott were connected. And so were Mia and Lucas.

Still, she kept that bit of information to herself.

"So now that I can do what I can do, what's the plan?" Scott asked.

She noticed that he was slurring his words. They had skipped dinner, and he was on his second glass of wine. She'd only ever seen him drunk twice and figured he was due tonight. They all were. They had achieved what they had come here for.

She knew how to take them all with her to the Beyond, and Scott could now transform into a dog, along with Lucas and Mia.

"Now, we wait. The next full moon is less than a week from now." Lucas poured himself more wine.

Mia stood up and walked into the kitchen. She came back with a bag of crackers, some cheese, and a jar of jelly. She returned a second time with chips and salsa.

Everyone scooted around the coffee table and snacked, drank, and plotted.

"Why is Moros talking to us?" Scott asked sometime later. "Why now?" He shook his head, needing to understand.

"Your power has grown today," Lucas answered. "You're getting attention now. The three of us, four," he corrected with a wave of his glass, "are very powerful."

Selene glanced around. "Tara..." Everyone turned to her. "The others. They said that everyone in Hidden Creek had drawn attention because of their joined power. She called it a pulse that can be felt by those of power."

A pulse. That's what the four of them were. A heartbeat moving at the same pace towards the same goal—keeping the world alive.

The next day, they all trained together. They took turns sparring, three on one. When it was Mia's turn, Lucas was the only one who actually touched her. Not that he hit her. He just stopped inches from her nose and playfully tapped the end of it with one finger, which seemed to piss Mia off.

Suddenly, the two of them were fighting one another while Scott and Selene watched from a distance.

"Do you think they know?" Selene whispered to him.

"Hm?" he asked, trying to keep track of who was winning.

"That they like one another." She nudged his shoulder.

"Who? Them?" He almost laughed. Then he frowned. "Damn. Why didn't I see it before now?"

Selene chuckled. "I doubt they even see it." She sighed. "I'm hungry. How about we break for lunch?"

"Can't, until Mia lets us out of here." He glanced around at the odd-colored world.

"Right." Selene frowned. "Should we interrupt them?"

He shook his head. "Nope, I'm too afraid of Mia."

Selene chuckled. "Yeah, my brother doesn't scare me as much she does. Not after sparring with Mia. I got this close" —she held her fingers an inch apart from one another–"to actually touching her during our last fight. She's fast."

"You've improved since we've gotten here." He turned to Selene. She looked happier than he could ever remember her being before. He felt a whole lot happier than when they had first arrived as well.

He pulled her into his arms and kissed her until the warmth of her spread throughout every part of his body.

"Get a room," Mia said, storming past them. Then she

snapped her fingers, and they were out of the Between. "It's lunchtime."

"She's just upset because I won," Lucas said with a smile as he walked by them.

"Did not," Mia called back.

Lucas glanced over his shoulder and winked and nodded at them.

"I saw that," Mia said as she climbed the deck stairs.

Selene glanced over at Scott, and they couldn't help but chuckle as they strolled inside together.

"Now that the training part of our trip is over, I guess we need to strategize some more. I still feel like we're going into this blind," Scott said as they ate.

"We all are," Mia agreed. She looked to Lucas, who frowned into his beer.

"There is nothing more I can tell you. Everything in the... Beyond is shielded from me." He glanced up at Selene. "I can only see the four of us traveling there and what skills we need for the desired outcome."

Everyone soaked that bit of information in.

"Then we go in blind," Scott said. "We have the skills we need." He glanced over at Selene. "That's got to count for something. Right?"

"I could look?" Mia suggested. "See if I can see anything you don't have the skills to," she said in Lucas' direction.

Lucas frowned. "I have the skills, it's hidden from me," he retorted.

Mia waved her hand like she was dismissing a child.

"How can you look?" Selene asked.

"It's sort of a ritual," Mia answered. "We'll have to start at midnight."

"What? Like a séance?" Selene asked with a half chuckle.

"Something like that," Mia said with a solemn look.

"Okay, I'm game," Selene said eagerly. When he looked at her with an are-you-serious look, she shrugged. "I've always wondered if they were real."

"So, we have a ritual." Lucas stood up to take his dish to the kitchen. "I have a few calls to make," he said, and then disappeared.

"He's still sore I kicked his ass," Mia joked.

"I would think that the CEO of a large corporation had a few hours of business he had to tend to each day," Scott said with a shrug. "I'm just thankful he's giving me the time off."

He *was* thankful. Every day he checked his emails and calls, and every day he found most of his work had already been handled. Everyone in the office assumed that he was on a retreat with the boss. They wondered how he'd gotten lucky enough to meet the man in the first place. Most of them asked if this meant he was getting a raise when he returned.

At this point, Scott was just hoping that they would survive the next few days.

After lunch, they all disappeared into their separate rooms or different corners of the big house. He followed Selene down to their room. While she lay on the bed, scrolling through her phone, he clocked in on his laptop and checked messages.

He hadn't meant to fall asleep, and when he heard Selene crying, he jerked awake.

She was asleep next to him, her body curled tight into a ball. In her sleep, tears rolled down her cheeks as soft whispers escaped her lips.

Setting his laptop aside, he gathered her in his arms.

"It's so cold," she murmured.

How many nightmares had he comforted her about over the years?

He wasn't one to complain about the past. Yes, their lives had been hell. Yes, they'd suffered and had gone to bed cold, hungry, or scared on more than a handful of occasions.

He hadn't suffered with nightmares. Selene had.

The older she got, the worse they seemed to be. Now, as he held her against his chest, she seemed to relax and calm down.

Her tears soaked his T-shirt as he glanced towards the windows. It was dark outside. How late was it?

He didn't want to move to look since she'd finally settled back asleep. Or so he'd thought.

"Thank you," she said a few moments later. "I didn't mean to wake you." She shifted to look up at him.

"It's okay." He brushed his hand down her hair, stroking the soft tresses and enjoying the feel and smell of her against him.

"We were at Shelly's," she said, and he winced.

"That was a shithole." He pulled her tighter.

"I'd just learned how to fly." She sighed and rested her head against his shoulder. "You'd just joined the basketball team."

He remembered. Remembered the crush he'd had on Jenny Lipton, one of the cheerleaders. Jenny was nice enough to share her lunches with him since most days they went without.

It was the first year he'd put Selene's well-being and needs aside for his own. In an extremely selfish act, he'd let her fend for herself most evenings.

He'd believed she was safe since Shelly Lenard was drunk most of the time and ignored them.

That had lasted until the night he'd come home early from practice and found Selene in the hall closet. Shelly was passed out drunk on the sofa, her large dress hanging off her as if she'd been in a fight.

He hadn't known what Selene had been going through in the past year. Not until that night. He'd spent most of his time away at basketball practice and jumping from party to party with Jenny that year.

When Scott had found Selene locked in the hall closet, she was tied up with the vacuum cleaner cord and gagged with a large dirty rag.

After untying her, he'd packed up their stuff and had stolen Shelly's truck and driven back to the home, where one of the workers had called the police.

Shortly after that, they were placed with the Lindseys, and everything had changed for them. He had changed.

His life was no longer just his. He had failed Selene, and he swore he would never do that again.

"Yeah," he said now. He kissed the top of her head as the weight of everything that had happened to her, the hell she had lived through while he had been trying to get laid for the first time, had the guilt stinging all over again. "I remember."

She shifted until she was looking up at him. "It wasn't your fault."

His fingers were still tangled in her hair. He nudged her closer until their lips met.

"Yes, it was." He pulled her body over his as his hands roamed over her hips. "I won't let anything like that happen to you again."

"Is that why you're here?" she asked, straddling him.

"I'm here for you," he said with a groan as her body moved over his. Her thighs were brushing against his hips. Her pussy rubbed across his cock. Even though they were fully clothed, he felt on the edge. All it would take was her touching him, skin against skin, and he'd lose the hold on his self-control.

"Scott," Selene purred.

"Hm?" He opened his eyes and focused on hers.

She ran her eyes over him slowly, appearing as if she wanted to say something, then she leaned down and kissed him until he forgot everything.

CHAPTER FIFTEEN

At midnight, the four of them gathered in the downstairs living room. There was a fire in the fireplace, and Mia set a bunch of candles around the room and lit them.

She'd pulled the coffee table and sofa and chairs out so they could all sit in a circle, cross-legged, in the middle of the floor.

Rain had started shortly before dinner and now there was a full-blown storm outside.

"Seriously? I can't believe we're doing this on a night like this. All week long, no rain. The night we decide to hold a séance..." Scott motioned to the large glass doors. "Freaky."

"It's not bad," Selene said, taking Scott's hand.

"Doesn't it freak you out? I mean..." He motioned to the candles, the fire, then the doors when lightning flashed outside.

Selene smiled. "I guess just knowing I've been traveling to hell all my life makes things like this less scary." She shifted and squeezed his hand, then reached over and took Lucas's hand.

Scott took Mia's and then Mia and Lucas closed the circle.

"No talking. And no matter what, don't break the circle," Mia warned. "Let me be clear—this isn't one of those fake warnings." Her eyes traveled around to each of them. "Do not, under any circumstance, break this." She held up her hands. "Understand?" Each of them agreed.

She had placed the largest candle in the middle. It was one of those large ones that had three wicks in it, and it sat in a massive clay bowl.

As Mia closed her eyes and started talking in a low tone, the flames started dancing. Each of them watched a flame while Mia's eyes stayed closed.

Selene felt as if she could disappear into the fire. She watched it dance, letting Mia's soft voice lull her.

She blinked. Or thought she did. Her body shifted slightly. She felt the ground under her move. Then, suddenly, the four of them were... somewhere else.

Loud moans. Cries. People in pain. Screams. There was so much darkness. So much... heat.

She jerked once, but Lucas held her hand firmly. She couldn't tear her eyes from the flame.

She felt Scott's hand jerk in hers, but his grip tightened.

"Hold on. Don't speak." Mia's voice echoed in her mind.

In the corner of her eyes, Selene could see a shadow approach them. The screams seemed to grow louder.

"What is this, Imp?" a voice hissed directly behind Selene. "Have you brought us snacks?"

Mia's voice rose. "Be gone, daemon. We have no use for you."

There was a loud cackling sound. "You think you have any authority here?" the hiss came.

"I have all the authority," Mia said. "Do you see whom I've come with?"

There was silence. "How have you come across this child?"

"She is under my protection," Mia answered, and Selene felt a shiver race through her.

"She belongs here. Give her to us. We will protect her."

"Tell us what we need to know," Mia said. "Then we can talk."

Selene frowned, but since her eyes were locked on the flame, she couldn't look up to see if Mia was telling the truth. She doubted it, but still...

"What truth do you seek?"

"Moros. Does he still slumber?"

"Yes."

"And Elpis?"

"Yes."

It was quiet for a moment. "For how long?" Mia asked.

The shadow chuckled, the sound a mixture of hissing and cackling.

"You ask the right questions, Imp."

"You haven't answered my last question."

"Years, days, hours, what do I know of those worldly things."

"Hades?" The moment Mia said the name, everything around them seemed to stop. The sounds. The wind. The heat.

"Our master will know of your visit. He will hear of your keeping the girl from her place. Each time she is here, his power grows. He will come for you and make you pay, Imp."

"Then I take it he still slumbers too," Mia said casually.

The sounds started up again. "I have answered your questions. Release our child to us."

"One last question," Mia said, causing the creature to hiss so loudly behind her that Selene almost broke the connection.

"Asskk."

"Three hellhounds it takes to hold the gate. Three hellhounds must be present to wake the Fates," Mia chanted. "Are we the three that are called to be?"

There was silence and then laughter. "No, Imp. What I see before me are mere pups. Powerful, yes, especially the three that are bonded with blood. But to call upon the Fates, you will need a star." There was a pause. "No, set the child free. She has much to do here, along with her sister."

"I think we'll hold onto her for a while longer," Mia said and quickly broke the connection, sending them spiraling around so quickly that Selene felt her stomach lurch. Then, with a thud, the four of them landed back on the floor on the soft carpet.

All but one candle was extinguished. The three-flame candle was burned clear down to the last of the wicks.

"That was fun," Lucas said, moving to stand up.

"Um, you might want to..." Mia started, but she wasn't fast enough and ended up having to catch Lucas. "We've been gone for a while," she said as Lucas sat on the edge of the coffee table and rubbed his legs.

"A while?" he asked.

Mia leaned over and took up her phone. "Two days," she said with a wince.

"What?" Lucas barked. "We were gone for two days?"

"That would mean that the full moon is in two nights," Selene said softly.

Everyone turned to her.

"Why did time pass differently this time? Whenever we went before, it was as if we hadn't left," Scott asked.

Mia bit her bottom lip. "There was a theory that a shift of power can cause a flux. I suppose that could be the reason. I've never taken so many with me before, so I'm just spitballing here," she added with a shrug.

"Does that mean when we go next time this will happen again?" Selene asked.

"There is that possibility. Things have... changed. Power is being woken by our trip. The next time we will be in the flesh. This time was only our projections. I can't be sure what will happen," Mia answered.

"You mean, our bodies stayed here?" Scott asked looking down at his legs as he rubbed them.

"Yes, which is why every part of me feels asleep," Mia joked.

"What did we learn?" Scott asked. "I didn't really understand any of that.

"First, food," Mia said, rubbing her legs. "Scratch that. First, bathroom. Then food." She stood up. "Stretch your legs before you try standing."

Mia walked out of the room. Lucas followed her, leaving Selene and Scott alone, still sitting on the floor.

"Why did that thing want me?" she asked softly.

Scott took her hand and squeezed it lightly.

"Selene, goddess of the moon and the Beyond," Scott said in a low tone, causing a shiver to race up her spine.

"If I'm the goddess of all that, why did it seem as if that thing wanted me for another reason?" she asked.

"It mentioned three that were bonded with blood," Scott pointed out.

"Tara, Lucas, and I." Selene sighed.

"How about we head upstairs and let Mia explain the rest of it?" Scott suggested.

He helped her stand up, and after they used the bathroom, they headed upstairs.

Mia was in the kitchen, cutting cheese slices into small squares. There was tray of meat already cut into pieces on a large platter.

"Charcuterie night," Mia said with a slight cheer. "Selene, why don't you pour the wine?" She motioned to the bottles sitting on the table. "Scott, you can get the crackers." She nodded to the pantry.

By the time Lucas appeared, they had the table full of finger foods.

"There he is," Mia cheered. "You aren't still mad at me, are you? I had no clue we'd be gone two days." She rolled her eyes.

"I had a lot of explaining to do," Lucas said. "If anyone asks, we were on a hike in a remote area," he said to Scott. "A team building type of thing." He rolled his eyes. "Oh, and you're the new regional manager for Atlanta."

Scott choked on the sip of wine he'd just taken. "What?"

Lucas shrugged and sat down next to Mia and started filling his plate with food. "It was that or tell them what was going on. Besides, Robert Kline is an ass and I've been wanting to sack him for a while."

Scott glanced over at Selene. She smiled at him. "Congrats," she said, holding up her wine.

Scott shook his head and tapped his glass to hers.

"Now, how about you explain what the hell just happened," Lucas said to Mia.

"In a nutshell, the three of us"—Mia motioned to her, Lucas, and Scott—"are basically lapdogs." She shrugged.

"Either the daemon was lying or..." She let the rest of the sentence hang.

"So, your plan failed." Scott turned to Lucas.

"No, not necessarily. What I saw could still be beneficial. If not temporary." Lucas was frowning.

"What does that mean?" Selene asked.

"It means, we go ahead with our plan. Tomorrow, you take us to the Beyond," he said, and she smiled a little inside knowing that he finally thought of it as that instead of the Underworld.

"And what? Hope that our plan works?" Scott asked.

"It will work," Lucas said firmly. "I've seen it."

"Okay, so we go. Then what? What if all this is just... a Band-Aid?" Mia asked.

"Then it is, and we regroup," Lucas said easily. "At least we will have kept Moros from destroying everything for another day."

"Okay," Selene said after a long silence. "Now, can I ask... What the fuck? Why did the daemon want me? Why does he think Hades' power grows stronger while I'm there?"

Everyone turned to Mia.

"Because it does," Lucas said, gaining everyone's attention. "The story goes that Hades kidnapped the goddess Persephone from Sicily and took her to the Underworld so he could marry her."

"What has that got to do with me?" Selene asked.

"Gods never die," Mia said softly, causing Lucas to nod.

"Selene, you're the goddess of darkness," Lucas said, as if that made everything clear. "Persephone was the goddess of the Underworld. It could be perceived as one and the same."

Selene felt her stomach lurch. "I am not marrying the devil."

Scott took her hand as Mia and Lucas laughed.

"No," Lucas said. "That isn't what he wants. He needs you there for his power to grow. Which is why, after you drop us off, you need to leave."

"But I've been going to the Beyond all my life." She frowned.

"It's different," Mia said.

"What is?" Selene asked.

"You know the difference between the Void and the Between?" Mia asked.

"Yes," Selene said slowly.

"Your Beyond and the place we went today are two different places. Think about it," Mia said.

Suddenly, Selene knew it was true. Her safe haven was nothing like the loud, scary place they had all four just traveled to.

"Then, I haven't been going to the right place. I can't take you there," she said to Lucas. "But Mia can."

Mia shook her head. "It may have appeared as if we were there earlier, but we weren't. We were only a projection. Which is why our legs were stiff and we were hungry. I don't have the ability to take anyone anywhere."

"You take us to the Void and the Between," Selene pointed out.

"Those belong to me," Mia said. "I come from them. You come from..."

"The Underworld," Selene finished softly.

"We have two days to figure this out," Scott said, touching her arm. "For now, let's finish eating and get some rest."

They finished the meal in silence and then went their

separate ways. She and Scott lay in bed, listening to one another breathe, until Scott fell asleep.

When she knew that he was out, she pulled herself free from his arms and tiptoed out onto the balcony.

In the time they had been gone, the weather had changed. Thankfully, now it was warmer than it had been. She moved further away from the house and then turned and looked at the building.

Everything she loved was there. Everything except Tara.

Sitting in the tall grass, she closed her eyes and sent a mental message to her sister, telling her that she was working on coming back to Hidden Creek. That she was well. That she loved her. She hoped that Tara would receive it.

She opened her eyes again, then she concentrated as hard as she could, trying to remember every detail about the Underworld. About the place she'd barely seen as her eyes had been glued to the flames.

"Well, well," the same hissing voice said right next to her.

This time, she jerked her gaze around and stared at the daemon. It was a massive black and silver creature that, normally, she would have described as angelic looking. It had long silver wings that stretched out as tall as trees. Its body was so black it caused no light to bounce from it. She couldn't tell if it was naked or even if it was male, for that matter. In its right hand, it held a rope. Attached to that rope were more than a dozen people, dangling from their feet. Their screams were so loud, Selene wanted to cover her ears. In its left hand, it held a cage full of more people.

As she watched, it set the cage down on the ground.

This world was nothing like her Beyond, which was full

of dull but beautiful colors. Here, everything was charred and black or gray.

"We knew you would return," the daemon hissed as it bowed its head to her in some sort of act of respect.

"Who are you?" she asked.

"Erebus. I guard the place of darkness between the Underworld and the worlds," it answered. "I am darkness, and you are one of my masters." It bowed its large head again.

Her eyes kept returning to the humans in pain. "Who are they?" she asked, motioning.

Erebus glanced down at the cage and the people dangling from the rope. The fact that none of them called to her for help or stopped wailing in pain didn't go unnoticed.

"They are the lost. I am taking them to the river where they will travel to the gates," Erebus answered.

Selene frowned. They were the lost? As in souls? Damned souls. She felt a shiver up her spine.

"If I tell you to release them, what will happen?" she asked.

Erebus didn't balk at her question. Instead, he simply answered, "They will spread from here like a plague and infect the living worlds, always searching for a way back to the river so they may be judged."

Okay, so they were better off where they were, screaming and basically being tortured.

"What do I need to do to stop Moros?" she asked.

Erebus shook its head. "You? Nothing, my goddess."

She grew frustrated. "How do we stop Moros?"

"Only Elpis can stop Moros," Erebus answered.

"How do we find Elpis?"

"Pandora will waken Elpis when it is time."

"Why does my brother believe we need to be here in two days?" she asked.

Here Erebus paused. "The Fates must be summoned. They will show the path to Pandora, who was trapped in a realm. A great distance will need to be traveled. A price must be paid."

Erebus bent and picked up the cage again. "By coming here, in the flesh, you have caused the first lock to be unchained. Two more will need to be unchained before they can be summoned."

She frowned and suddenly felt an urgency to leave.

"What happens when I leave here?" she asked.

Erebus started walking away from her and said over its shoulder. "You have done what you came to do. Go. The next time you come, all will be revealed. As it has in the past and will be in the future."

Selene willed herself back to the field. When she felt the tall grass under her feet, she gasped as strong arms wrapped around her.

"Where the hell were you?" Scott said next to her ear as he held onto her.

It was then that she noticed it was daylight out. How long had she been gone?

CHAPTER SIXTEEN

"You were gone for over eight hours," Scott said. The words ground out as he pulled back the anger and worry that had fueled him the last eight hours since he'd woken up and found her gone. "We searched everywhere for you. You left without a word. Without telling anyone where you were going. What you were doing."

Selene winced. "I... thought I'd only be gone for a few moments."

"I did warn you that time could move differently in the Underworld now that things have shifted," Mia said.

The four of them were gathered once more in the kitchen, this time for lunch.

Selene was eating a sandwich and drinking a large glass of orange juice.

"What I found out was well worth it." She filled them in on what the daemon named Erebus had told her.

"It seemed very keen on answering my questions, so I got as much from it as I could."

"Erebus?" Lucas said, getting everyone's attention. He

was on his laptop and read off the basics from old Greek mythology. Nothing really seemed to fit, with the exception of the creature being darkness. "Is this the same creature you spoke to?" Lucas asked Mia.

Mia shrugged. "I didn't see it. There was only darkness surrounding us."

"Yes," Selene said, "it was the same." Then she frowned. She turned to Mia. "What did you mean when you said, 'Three hellhounds it takes to hold the gate. Three hellhounds must be present to wake the Fates. Are we the three that are called to be?'"

Everyone waited for Mia to answer.

"It's an old rhyme from my family. Loosely translated over the years. All djinns are taught it and told that it will either be their savior or their doom."

Scott felt Selene shiver next to her.

"Why don't you finish your food, then we'll go get some rest. If you left shortly after I fell asleep, that means you haven't slept yet," he suggested.

Selene stood up and took the rest of her sandwich with her as they started out. She stopped just at the top of the stairs. "At least I know one thing now," she said to the room. "I can bring the three of you to the Underworld and you will summon the Fates, who will answer the next part of this riddle."

He took her hand in his and led her down the stairs to their room.

She set the plate with her half-eaten sandwich down, and he shut the bedroom door and leaned against it. He watched her as she sat on the edge of the bed and removed her shoes.

He wanted to yell at her. To tell her how stupid of a move that was. But he couldn't. She'd done it to get more answers and had done a better job at it than Mia had. Still, he hated that she had put herself in danger without telling anyone.

"I can hear you berating me in your head from over here," Selene said, lying on the bed fully clothed.

He moved to sit next to her, not wanting to touch her. Not trusting that he wouldn't wrap his arms around her and never let go.

Selene pulled his arm until he lay beside her stiffly. Then she wrapped her body around his.

"Yell at me later, will you? I'm tired and just want to hold you," she said with a yawn.

He lay beside her silently until she fell asleep. Then he remained there, wishing more than anything that he could tell her just how he felt about her. In all the years they'd known one another, he'd never told her that he loved her. Not as a brother or in any other sense.

He lost track of time watching the shadows move across the ceiling of the room. By the time Selene shifted and started to wake, he had decided that he would tell her just what she meant to him. How she made him feel. But first, he wanted to show her.

Pulling her closer, he started trailing kisses over her face, her lips, her neck. He felt her wake a little more with each kiss.

He peeled her clothes aside, pulled them off her lax body, then quickly tossed his off before sliding into her heat. No fuss. No foreplay other than the soft kisses he'd used to wake her.

"Scott," Selene sighed as she wrapped around him. Her arms. Her legs. Every part of her took him in. Completed him.

When they once again were lying in each other's arms, he closed his eyes.

"I love you," he whispered so softly that he wondered if she could hear him.

She stiffened and then sat up.

"You can't," she said, quickly looking around the room for her clothes.

"Why can't I?" he asked with humor as he watched her.

"Because you deserve better," she threw over her shoulder.

His smile fell. "What does that mean?"

She stopped pulling on her pants to look at him. Her eyes ran over him slowly, and he could see the desire clearly behind them. She waved her hand in his direction. "It means you deserve some sort of normalcy. I should have sent you back to the city. You could be flirting with Stacie."

"Who?" He frowned.

Selene rolled her eyes. "After this is over, you'll go back to Atlanta, and I'll go to Hidden Creek."

"Why? Why can't we go somewhere together?" He got out of the bed. He needed to hold her. To try and convince her this was the best plan.

"In a few hours, I'm going to deliver the three of you to the Underworld. Then it will be over. This will be over." She motioned between them.

"There is no way I'm going back to the way things were before." He stormed over to take her shoulders in his hands.

She easily jerked free and, for the first time in a long time, he remembered just how strong she was.

"You don't have a choice." She pulled on her shirt and left the room before he could get dressed and follow her.

By the time he did get dressed and went looking for her, everyone else was gathered in the living room upstairs.

"We leave in an hour," Lucas told them.

"Already?" Scott frowned as he watched Selene's face. She was avoiding his eyes. Avoiding him. "I thought we had another night?"

"Remember, time moves differently in the Underworld," Mia said with a frown. "It hadn't dawned on me that we'd need to leave early until Selene came back. We're eight hours away from when we need to be there. We have to leave in the next hour."

Scott moved over to Selene and put a protective hand on her shoulder. Thankfully, she didn't jerk away from him.

"What do we need?" Scott asked.

They all turned to Lucas.

"Nothing. Nothing we take with us will help in any way," he said. "I suggest we eat something to keep our strength up."

Everyone turned to him, since it was technically still his job to make dinner. He groaned and moved to find something quick to make.

"I'll help you," Mia said, joining him in the kitchen while Selene and Lucas moved further into the living room to talk.

He and Mia worked around the kitchen. He ended up making grilled cheese and turkey sandwiches while she put a large salad and dessert together.

They worked fast since there was less than forty minutes to go.

They had just set all the food on the bar top when Selene's raised voice had them looking into the other room.

"No, you can't," she said loudly. Her arms were crossed over her chest as she glared at Lucas.

Lucas said something in a low voice to Selene that

caused her to grow even angrier. She glanced over at him, as if he was what they were arguing about.

"Problems?" he asked, setting down the bowl and making his way towards them.

"No," Lucas said firmly. "Let's eat."

Scott stopped next to Selene. "Problems?" he asked softly.

"No," she said, walking past him.

He wanted to argue, to get to the bottom of their fight, but Mia called out that they had less than fifteen minutes to eat and head out.

They ate in silence, as if it was their last meal. He couldn't help glancing between Selene and Lucas the entire time. The two of them avoided each other's gazes.

"We can do dishes later," Mia said, checking her watch. When Selene moved to grab a coat, Mia added, "You won't need that."

Selene shrugged and then followed everyone outside. Scott followed Selene.

"Is this going to be an issue?" Lucas asked Selene.

"No," she answered quickly. Then she glared at Lucas.

"What the hell is the problem with the two of you?" Mia turned on them. "We have about five minutes, and I refuse to take another step before you clear the air."

Selene glanced at Scott then back at Mia.

"Lucas thinks that I should leave the three of you there. I told him that Erebus didn't seem to care if I stayed or went. I doubt it will matter. Besides, how are you supposed to get back?" Selene asked, talking quickly.

"I agree," Mia said. "Selene stays." She turned to Lucas, who opened his mouth to argue. "She stays," Mia said a little firmer.

"Fine," Lucas growled out. "We change before we go." He nodded to the others.

Scott willed his form to change. The first few times he'd done it, he'd practically hyperventilated. Now, it was as easy as snapping his fingers.

He felt his body grow, change, twist. Then he was staring down at Selene from almost ten feet. Mia and Lucas stood shoulder to shoulder next to him. In this form, his eyesight was far better than anything he'd experienced before. He could smell things he'd never smelled before, even from miles away. Things deep down in the earth. Things in the air and the trees. Selene. He held on to the smell of her as the world around them twisted and bent.

Selene. He would remember her no matter what.

Darkness came moments later. Along with pain. So much pain. He felt as if his sides were on fire.

When they appeared in a place he had never seen, a place filled with all new scents and sounds, he almost fell flat on his face.

"Steady," Lucas growled out.

"What the..." Mia said at the same time he did as she jerked her head towards him, banging her snout against his.

Selene stood in front of them, sober. Then she burst out laughing.

"We have to work together," Lucas said.

"Did you know this would happen?" Mia asked.

"I had an idea," Lucas replied.

It was then that Scott looked down at the two massive paws underneath the three of them.

"Shit," he said when he realized the three of them had merged into a three-headed dog roughly the size of a barn.

"I guess I should have guessed," Mia said with a sigh. "We're Cerberus."

"No, but we're doing a smashing job of looking like him. Now, we have a long way to travel and not enough time," Lucas said. "I'll do the steering." He took a step but stopped, then looked down at Selene. "Coming?"

Selene frowned up at them. "Yes, how?"

Lucas raised a paw. "Climb aboard."

"This is so weird," Mia said when they were jogging across a black field with Mia on their back.

"Hey," Lucas said, when Mia bumped into him. "Just… relax. Like you're in the passenger seat. Let me do the driving."

Scott did as Lucas suggested, letting his mind wander as they ran through field after field, over more than a dozen hills. He supposed they could have been mountains. The landscape was so odd, he couldn't tell.

Instead of normal trees and rocks, everything around them were just shapes, like nothing had formed completely.

Then they came upon a river. It appeared much like the one Selene had shown him in her Beyond place. The red water flowed so slowly, he questioned if it moved at all.

"The Styx," Mia said.

"The gates are just beyond here," Lucas said.

"Gates?" Selene asked.

"There are many paths to hell," Mia supplied.

"Here is where we part," Lucas told Selene.

"No, I go the entire way," she said firmly. "This is my place."

"Scott, talk some sense into her," Lucas said.

Scott thought about it but, in truth, he didn't want to lose sight of Selene. The thought of leaving her here while they went ahead scared him.

"I'm coming," Selene said more firmly.

"Let her come," Scott suggested.

Lucas was quiet for a moment.

"How are we going to cross the river?" Mia asked. "There's the ferryman, but…"

"There is no ferryman," Lucas said. "Never was. That was a myth."

"Okay, so…" Mia asked.

"This is why Selene needs to stay here. Because we swim across. No mortal soul can survive the water outside of the forms we took."

"If we aren't really Cerberus, how do you know we'll survive?" Scott asked.

"There's one way to find out." Lucas moved closer to the water and raised a paw towards the water. As he lowered it, the ground shifted and moved, forming some type of stepping stone of black dirt.

"Guess you don't have to swim after all," Selene said sarcastically. "Which means I go."

Lucas growled and continued to move across the river quickly.

Just past the edge of the river was a road of sorts. Here, there were lines and lines of shadow creatures. There must have been millions of them, each line as long as the eye could see.

"They march to the gates," Mia said.

"How do we get through?" Selene asked.

But once again, the moment Lucas moved forward, the way parted. The dark shadows moved aside as if they were water.

Lucas started walking slowly ahead. The shadows closed around them, only parting for a few feet ahead of each step.

It seemed like hours later when a large structure appeared ahead.

"The gate," Mia said, and Scott felt a shiver race through their joined bodies.

"Sorry," Mia joked. "Still, it's spooky as hell."

"It is hell," Lucas reminded her.

"Yeah, something to write home about," Mia said dryly.

The closer they got, the clearer it became how large the gate was. Finally, they stood at the base of the massive structure. It looked nothing like Rodin's sculpture depicting the gate, which he'd seen a picture of once.

It was almost a hundred stories high with two large black spikes on either side. Along each spike, snake-like creatures twisted and turned, opening and closing the gate as each shadow passed through.

It was far more beautiful than Scott would have imagined.

"Now what?" Mia asked.

Selene shifted and stood on their back when they came to the base of the gate. "Now I do my thing."

"I call upon the Fates," Selene said loudly. "So that they may answer a question."

A banging sound echoed so intensely that Selene almost fell off them.

The gates shut and remained so for almost an entire minute.

"Did it work?" Mia asked.

Suddenly, the doors opened, and the shadows moved back as three women stepped forward.

Once they were outside, the gate shut silently behind them.

The women peered at Selene, standing high on the dog's back.

The women were dressed in long black robes that clung to their bodies. He'd always imagined the Fates as old, hag-like creatures. Instead, beautiful fair-haired women of around twenty years old stood before them, each with different brightly colored eyes.

CHAPTER SEVENTEEN

"What trickery is this?" the yellow-eyed women asked, her voice echoing loudly across the space.

"They think they can deceive us," the red-eyed one said as they all moved closer to them.

Selene felt the dog that was her three friends shift under her.

"Steady," she heard Lucas say.

"An impressive feat. It is an impressive feat that they have made it this far," the green-eyed one said, stepping forward. "I am Clotho. Spinner of life."

"And I am Lachesis, dispenser of life." The yellow-eyed woman stepped forward.

"I am Atropos, ender of life." The red-eyed woman smiled as she stepped forward.

"What is it you want of us, child of darkness?" Clotho asked Selene. Selene turned her eyes to the woman.

"We seek a way to bind Moros," Selene told the three of them.

The three women laughed. "You cannot bind him," Lachesis answered.

"Moros slumbers," Atropos said. "For now," she added with a cackle.

"He knocks on the door," Clotho said, just as a loud echo rang out. "You cannot bind him. It is fated."

"We're here to stop him," Lucas said.

The women's eyes narrowed as they all hissed. Then Atropos flicked her wrist in disapproval and Mia, Lucas, and Scott reverted back to their human forms. Selene plunged towards the ground. She screamed and was halfway to the ground when she remembered she could fly. Her scream stopped and she touched down gracefully next to Scott.

All three women looked at her with pleasure.

"You are of us," Atropos said. Then they turned to Mia and narrowed their eyes.

"You are not welcome here, djinn." Clotho raised her hand.

"No!" Selene cried out. She moved to block Mia from the Fates just as Lucas moved to do the same. "She stays. I am her protector."

"We are," Lucas said.

The Fates ran their eyes over Lucas. "You too, are of us," Atropos said.

That left Scott, standing by himself, a few feet from Selene. When the Fate's eyes rested on him, they immediately took a giant step back.

"You did not tell us you brought the spawn of Moros," Clotho hissed.

"What have you done?" Lachesis cried out.

Just then, the knocking echoed again, much louder.

Selene turned towards Scott, and suddenly she realized that the loud banging wasn't coming from the gates behind the three Fates. Instead, it was coming from Scott. His entire body shook with the noise. He stood, as if a statue, frozen. He looked at her as if he was trying to apologize.

"Moros slumbers no more." Clotho raised her hands in fear and cried out as if in pain. "You have doomed us all."

Just then, a loud laughing sound echoed and bounced off the gates. "There is no stopping fate."

"Quickly, we must destroy the vessel." Atropos raised her hand towards Scott.

"No!" Selene, Scott, and Mia screamed at the same time. They moved between the three Fates and Scott.

"He is under our protection," Lucas said firmly.

"If you wish to save the son of Moros, you must take him to Elysium." Clotho pointed towards Lucas. "You must take him yourself since you are the only one who can carry him across the meadows." She pointed to the left.

"Now, go. Quickly. There is no time." Clotho lifted her hand just as another loud bang echoed from Scott. This time, it was so loud that Scott fell to his knees as a pulse of dark light circled him.

"Selene," Scott whispered. Selene rushed towards Scott, but Lucas was there first and gripped Scott, trying to help him stand.

"I'm sorry, sis. I fucked up. I'll fix this. I promise," Lucas said.

Selene watched in horror as Lucas gripped Scott and the pair of them shimmered before her eyes and disappeared.

"No!" she cried out, rushing to where they had just been. "What have you done with them?" She turned on the Fates.

The three women looked back at her with amusement.

"We have done nothing. Helios has taken Moros's spawn to Elysium," Lachesis said. "For now."

Atropos smiled. "When the time is right, you will all be together. If you wish to save him, you must become one, as we are." She motioned between the three Fates.

"Bring them back." Mia took a step forward.

"Do not speak to us, djinn. You are not of us," Atropos hissed. "Go back to where you came from." Atropos waved her hand as if shooing a fly, and Mia disappeared in a puff of sand and smoke.

"No!" Selene cried out and rushed to where Mia had just been. "What have you done with her?" she demanded.

"I have sent her back from where she came," Atropos said with a shrug. "She is, well, just not here." She smiled.

Selene glanced around and shook her head. She was all alone. Everyone she trusted was gone. "What now?" she asked under her breath.

Just then, Clotho stepped forward and laid a hand on Selene's shoulder. "You know what you need to finish the task. To bind Moros and call upon Pandora."

"Pandora. Where?" Selene asked.

"She will come to you. Soon. When the time is right," Clotho answered.

"Will she release Elpis?" Selene asked.

"Yes, but first, you must save your friend. You are but only one part, as I am one." Clotho looked towards the other Fates and suddenly, Selene understood. She needed Tara. She, Tara, and Lucas had to come together to save Scott. "Now go. The journey forward is long."

"Remember, child," Clotho started.

"Moros cannot take what does not belong to him," the three Fates said together.

Then Clotho raised her hand and, with a flick, Selene felt herself spiraling.

She landed in the field behind Mia's family house

with a thud. Her breath was knocked from her lungs, and she lay in the wet grass, under a full moon, and cried.

It was an hour before she could stand up and walk back into the empty house. She didn't know just how long she'd been gone until she found her cell phone and noticed all the missed calls.

She was hungry and, after showering and changing, made herself a cold sandwich. She moved as if on autopilot. Every muscle in her body ached for Scott.

Her mind screamed, desperate to know that he was okay. That she and the others hadn't screwed up. That Lucas would keep Scott safe until she and Tara could get there. Wherever there was.

What was Elysium? While she ate, she used her laptop to search and found a bunch of different myths.

Most said that it was a field or plain where heroes went to die. A place of perfect happiness.

That didn't sound so bad.

So why did the Fates want Lucas to take Scott there? Had they sent Scott there to die?

Either way, she needed her sister, and she needed her fast. The quickest way to get to Hidden Creek was to fly, but it was still an hour before dark, and she couldn't risk being seen. She bided her time by doing more research. She found out all she could on Elysium. On Moros. Pandora and Elpis.

Nothing else sprang out at her except that Elysium was said to be at the end of the Earth. Just where that was, eluded her. Still, she figured that with Tara's help, they could find it.

After sunset, Selene pulled on her backpack, zipped her leather jacket, and shot off into the night sky.

Since it was dark and she couldn't really make out any roads, she used her phone's GPS to guide her way.

The town of Hidden Creek was large enough that she could see the lights when she came up to the outskirts of town.

Then she noticed a new light in the middle of town and smiled at the brightly lit sign, Harvest Moon Family Restaurant.

Deciding not to chance anyone seeing her land, she set down in the back alley of a building two blocks down and walked the rest of the way.

She was cold, hungry again, and desperate to get back to Scott.

Everything he'd said, everything she hadn't, played over in her mind since she'd returned.

She should have told him that she loved him. She should have not cared that he deserved better than her. She should have...

She stepped into the brightly lit restaurant and saw Tara standing inside, holding a pitcher of water.

When Tara saw her, she smiled and walked over and hugged her. "You're back."

"I am, but not for long," Selene admitted. "I came back to get some help. Scott's been taken."

"Taken?" Tara gasped. "By whom?"

Selene felt her heart sink. "Our brother."

"Wait, what?" Tara shook her head. "We have a brother?"

"Yes." Selene glanced around. "Can you take a break?"

Tara looked around the crowded place. "Yes, but... How about you sit. I'll bring us something to eat and we can talk." Tara motioned towards an empty booth.

Selene walked over and sat down. Moments later, the

rest of the group she'd met last time she'd been in town were sitting at the table across from her.

"Oh, hey," she said, waving oddly. Everyone was just watching her.

"Are you okay?" Jessica asked.

"I..." She felt her throat close up and then, to her horror, she burst out crying.

Several people moved to her booth. None of them, thankfully, reached to touch her or hug her. Instead, they shielded her from the prying eyes of others. They waited and then listened to her relay the entire story. At one point, Tara sat down next to her and held Selene's hand while she talked.

When the entire story was out, including the bit about her not telling Scott she loved him, she felt drained. Soul and body.

"Here." Tara set a massive pile of fried chicken with mashed potatoes and white gravy in front of her.

"Comfort food," Tara said with a shrug as she dug into her own plate.

"What happens now?" someone asked.

Selene wiped the tears from her eyes and then picked up a chunk of chicken, dragged it through the potatoes and gravy, and took a bite.

"Now, Tara and I go to Elysium and, together with Lucas, we save Scott," she said between bites.

"How?" Tara asked. "How do we do that?"

"I can get us there," Selene answered.

"How?" Jess asked.

"The same way Brea can go places." Selene motioned to the couple sitting at the table near them. "Only, I can travel to the Underworld."

"Which is where Elysium is?" Tara asked, taking a sip of her water.

"Yes, it's... well, no. It's supposed to be at the end of the Earth," Selene answered.

"Which means?" Tara asked.

Selene set down the fork of potatoes she was about to shovel into her mouth. "Which means we try and, if we fail, we try again."

Tara glanced around. "I... I'll need to talk to Colt." She motioned towards the kitchen doors.

"Sure, I..." Selene started. "I need some rest first. I figured we'd go tomorrow night."

Tara nodded. "I'd better..." She motioned to the room, which was still full of customers.

"Sure. Great place, by the way." Selene smiled. "You guys did it."

Tara's smile grew. "Yes, we did."

CHAPTER EIGHTEEN

Beyond the pain, there was nothing. It was just the darkness and the pain. It shot through every fiber of his being. Bounced off every bone in his body. It was as if he were being ripped apart from the inside.

"Hold on." He heard Lucas's voice somewhere near him. "Almost there."

Scott could have sworn he was being carried. He felt the bouncing, but the pain was too strong, and he doubled over. He felt something trying to claw its way out of him and instantly guessed that it was Moros somehow. He was desperate to hold him back, deep inside him. He knew that if he didn't, he would never see Selene again.

Then there was a flash of light and all of the pain disappeared. He opened his eyes and realized Lucas was back in dog form and he was riding on his back.

The moment he opened his eyes, Lucas set him down and turned back into his human form.

"I guess that means we're here," Lucas said, looking around.

Scott saw where they were and gasped. They stood on a

white sandy beach. Before them, crystal-clear emerald waters spread out for as far as the eye could see.

Women of all shapes and sizes stood before them in white flowing gowns, sipping drinks.

When they were noticed, everyone turned to them and cheered. They were welcomed and ushered towards a covered pavilion that held a large fountain, where people sat around eating and drinking.

"What is this place?" Scott asked. "Why is my pain gone? What the hell was that anyway?" he asked Lucas.

"Short answers. This is Elysium, or paradise. Your pain is gone because, well, hello, we're in paradise. There is no pain here. And lastly, the pain was your father, Moros, trying to break free through you," Lucas answered.

"What?" He paused and turned to Lucas, who was smiling and sipping a drink.

"Don't worry. I'm going to fix this. But first, a toast." Lucas held up a glass, and one was shoved into Scott's hand. "Here's to hoping Selene will take a lifetime to come save us." He winked at Scott and then took a sip. "Damn, that's good."

Scott set his glass down, untouched. All he could think about was Selene. Even Lucas seemed to be preoccupied with something. Even though he flirted, drank, and ate, he continued to glance around as if waiting for something to happen.

This went on for... Scott had no idea how long. He lost track of time. Lost track of... well, everything. Time passed, but also it didn't. He and Lucas speculated that time was irrelevant here. Since there was technically no day or night, they couldn't tell if they'd been there an hour or a year. He supposed it was another trick of paradise to make its inhabitants more relaxed.

By his best guess, they had been there for a month now. Thirty long days and lonely nights without any word about Selene.

"Is this it then?" Scott asked Lucas.

"Not sure, bro." Lucas slapped him on the back.

The only good thing about being stuck in paradise was that he and Lucas had become close friends.

Lucas had filled him in on his childhood, while Scott had told him all about his and Selene's. It was as if Selene's brother wanted to know but had been too afraid to ask, so Scott just kept telling stories of their past. After a few days of that, Lucas had started opening up about his childhood.

He'd spent the first six years in an orphanage outside of Boston. Then he'd been adopted by Leslie and Leif Romano. They had moved into a large house in upstate New York, where he'd spent his childhood.

When it first became clear he was different, his parents had accepted his abilities and allowed him to explore them in a safe place. By the time he was in college, he'd learned who he could trust and who he couldn't.

Scott gathered there had been some hurt in his past, because he was very guarded about his college years and the time he'd spent working for his father's company before the older man retired and he took over.

"I spend most of my time in New York," Lucas said.

They were sitting in lounge chairs, sipping drinks while they watched a group of people play in the water in front of them.

"Is that where you'll be going back to once all this is over?" he asked.

Lucas glanced around. "Now, I'm not so—" Lucas stopped talking and stilled, then he smiled. "They're here." He set his drink down and stood up.

Scott jumped up, turned around, and saw Selene and Tara walking towards them.

He rushed towards her as she ran to him. They met in the middle of the sand.

Scott caught Selene and held on as she cried, and he took all of her in. Her smell, the feel of her against him. Everything.

"You're okay," she said as she rained kisses over him.

"I am," he said with a laugh.

Her body slid down his until her feet touched the soft sand.

"Please tell me you haven't been stuck in this place the entire time." Selene glanced around.

"We have," Lucas answered as he stopped beside them. "It's been pure hell," he joked.

Selene walked over to Lucas and hugged him.

Tara walked over to Scott and wrapped her arms around him. "I'm glad you're okay. Selene was really worried about you."

"It's good to see you again," he said.

"Tara, our brother Lucas." Selene motioned between the two.

Tara walked over and hugged Lucas. "I take it this means everything ended up, okay?"

"For now." Lucas motioned to Scott. "We still have the issue of Moros using Scott as a portal to escape his prison. If we leave here..."

Everyone looked over at him. "I need a drink." He walked over to where he'd set his down and drank the rest of it in one gulp.

He knew what Lucas was saying. If he stepped foot outside of Elysium, his father, who was the epitome of doom, would use him to break into the real world and destroy everything. Scott would die.

Selene walked over and took his hand. "Let's go somewhere to talk," she said softly.

He glanced over to where Tara and Lucas were walking towards a couple of chairs under a palm tree.

Scott pulled Selene into his arms and held onto her for another moment, then they started walking down the beach together.

"What is this place?" she asked after a few steps.

"Paradise." He smiled. "Lucas thinks that each person sees something different. I'm on a beach. He's at a top-dollar hotel in New York. Where are you?" he asked, turning to her.

"I'm on a beach too." She motioned to the water. "Clear emerald waters." She looked down. "White sand."

He nodded. "You're wearing a white flowing gown like everyone else."

She nodded. "You're in board shorts and a white shirt." She lifted her fingers to his chest. "I like the look on you."

"You look good in white," he told her.

"So, Lucas doesn't see the beach?"

"No, it took us a few days to figure that out. I mentioned something about what powers it took to keep the sand from getting everywhere and he looked at me like I was crazy," Scott said. "In his mind, we chill out each day by the pool instead of the beach."

"Wow." Selene shook her head as they started walking again.

"So, you like the beach?" he asked her, and she laughed.

"That trip to Orange Beach our senior year." She nodded. "This is that place."

"Yeah. The resort we walked by and snuck into after sunset." He smiled. "I'm sleeping in the best suite."

"So, while you've been living it up here"—she stopped and turned to him—"Tara and I have been doing some digging."

"And?"

"We think that when we leave here, we should take you to Hidden Creek, to the silo."

"Where they fought your parents?" he asked, remembering the place.

Selene nodded. "The rest of them are going to be there. Jess is pretty sure she and the others can bind your father."

"After he tears me apart?"

"No." Selene took his hands. "No, they think that it won't come to that."

"Think?"

"Ninety-nine percent sure," she lied with a weak smile. "If things go wrong, you and I return here and spend the rest of eternity living in paradise." She smiled.

What other choice did he have? Before, he'd felt a call to return to the real world. Now, with Selene here, he didn't mind where he was. But in truth, he still wanted a normal life. With her.

"Okay," he said with a nod. "Let's do this."

She took a deep breath. "Since I'm not sure how time moves differently, we have to send Lucas and Tara back first. Then Lucas can return to let us know when everyone is in position."

He nodded again, and they headed back to where her brother and sister were. "You have a family now," he said as they got closer.

Tara was laughing at something Lucas had said. They looked happy. Excited to finally get to meet.

"Yeah." Selene lifted their joined hands. "So do you."

"Sure. I have a dad that wants to rip me apart from the inside so he can doom the entire world," he joked.

Selene tugged on his hand to stop him. Instead of meeting his eyes, she looked at a spot on his chest.

"I should have told you how I feel," she said softly.

He nudged her chin up with his fingers until she looked at him. Until he could see deep into those dark chocolate eyes of hers. "Tell me now."

"I love you. I've always loved you," she said, causing his heart to skip a beat in his chest. Then she was crying, and it almost broke him. "I almost lost you before I had a chance to tell you that."

He pulled her into his arms. "I'm here," he said into her hair. "We'll make it through this, together."

"When this is all over, I want to move in with you," she said against his chest. "Wherever you want to live, it doesn't matter to me."

He smiled. "You know, Lucas and I have decided to open a new branch of Forge International."

Selene glanced up at him. "You have?"

He nodded. "I'll be the branch manager of the new Hidden Creek office."

Selene smiled. "I think we'd like living there."

"Let's find out." He took her hand. "But first, we have to deal with my father."

The four of them caught up and went over the plan a few times before Lucas and Tara disappeared to head back to Hidden Creek. Then he and Selene sat and waited for Lucas to return.

They didn't have to wait long. Within five minutes, Lucas was back.

"We're all ready. Despite what it seems, time is normal here," Lucas said. "Half an hour, everyone will be in place."

Selene took his hand and then took Lucas's. He closed the circle and, before anything else, leaned over and kissed Selene.

"I love you," he told her.

She smiled. "I love you."

"Let's do this." He held on as the sunny beach paradise disappeared and the three of them appeared at the base of a dark silo with the full moon overhead.

Instantly, the pain had him doubling over. Once again, he felt as if he was being ripped in two.

"Hold on to me," he heard Selene saying, just before everything went dark.

CHAPTER NINETEEN

Selene held onto Scott's hand as the rest of the group quickly joined in a large circle around them.

When she heard him scream, Selene wanted to rush to Scott, to pull him into her arms and escape back to the beach. Back to paradise.

Instead, she held onto him firmly as Jess and the other's started chanting loudly around them. They were saying something she couldn't understand.

She knew there was a chance that what they were doing wouldn't work. The spell to bind Moros that Jess had found in her book was a longshot at best.

They needed Elpis to undo the doom that was Moros. But first they needed Pandora to unleash Elpis.

Selene had agreed to try Jess's idea to save Scott only because she knew that, if things didn't work, she could snatch Scott away and whisk him back to Elysium in a heartbeat.

Thoughts of living with him there, in paradise, on the beach, played in her mind for a split second. She returned to the present when Scott doubled over and screamed in pain.

A large gust of wind kicked up in the silo, spinning like a tornado in the massive silo. Dirt, debris, and trash were lifted high over their heads, as if being sucked out of the silo.

The chanting from the rest of the group changed and grew louder. Jess stepped forward and pointed at Scott, then practically screamed something in a different language at him.

At that moment, a dark shadow flew from Scott's chest, and he almost fell backwards. If she and Lucas hadn't been holding him up, he would have. The shadow lifted high into the middle of the silo, floating almost thirty feet over their heads as they kept chanting. The wind increased.

"You seek to bind me?" A loud booming voice echoed in the silo. It emanated from the dark shadow. "Fools. You cannot bind a god. One whose path is already fated."

Scott stood up straight next to her, taking it all in, and she was at least thankful he no longer appeared to be in pain. The rest of the group chanted and held the circle firmly. Their words were drowned out by the loud laughter from Moros.

"I am the god of doom. I will take what I have created" —the shadow motioned towards Scott—and bring about the destruction of this world," Moros said.

"You have no hold on Scott," Selene yelled out, wanting to block its path back to Scott.

"Children of Rhea and Typhon, I will not destroy you or the other children of gods scattered around this place out of respect for my brethren," Moros said, ignoring her words. "But only if you leave this realm now and never return. This is your only warning."

Jess and the others continued chanting, their voices raising slightly higher.

"We're not going anywhere," Lucas yelled back.

"So be it," Moros said, and the shadow shifted downwards, back towards Scott.

"Leave Scott alone," Selene yelled, breaking the inner circle and stepping between the shadow and Scott.

"He is my creation alone. I made him for this purpose alone. I will take him and use him to bring about doom," Moros hissed.

"Not on my watch." Selene pushed herself up off the ground and plunged deep into the darkness. She vaguely heard Scott scream her name, but she was too far gone, fighting for what she loved. For the man she wanted to be with for the rest of her life.

She pushed through the darkness and was surprised to come up against something solid. She pushed back and fought as hard as she could against what appeared to be a creature made out of only arms.

So many hands pushed, shoved, and punched at her. Long nails scraped at her clothes and skin as she clawed her way through them, trying to hold back whatever Moros was, to keep him away from Scott.

Whatever she did, she had to keep Moros away from Scott.

She used all her strength, all her power, just to knock the thing back a foot.

Then she realized that she wasn't fighting Moros alone. Lucas and Tara were there, hovering next to her, thirty feet above everyone else.

Lucas was punching his way through the arms while Tara clawed at them.

She didn't know how long the three of them fought, but

she did know that it seemed to be futile. She was growing tired, and Moros was winning.

Tara was thrown from the smoke creature first. She flew backwards and landed on the floor. Next was Lucas. He hit a wall and then landed on the ground.

She fought for as long as she could by herself.

When Moros was less than five feet from Scott, he finally overtook her.

The chanting continued from the group, strengthened, growing louder until the silo practically shook.

It seemed to momentarily bind Moros, and Selene gathered all her strength for her next move. Then she remembered the Fate's last words to her.

"*Moros cannot take what does not belong to him.*"

Instead of using her strength to push back Moros, she changed tactics and turned to wrap her arms tightly around Scott. Scott held onto her in return.

"I love you," she said as tears rolled onto her cheeks. "From the moment we first met, I was yours."

"I love you too," Scott said. "From the first moment I saw you, I was yours." He kissed her.

"No!" Moros screamed behind them. "You cannot have him. He is mine! I need a solid pathway, a form I can possess that is of my making. One that belongs to me."

Selene jerked back from Scott and looked up at the god of doom.

"No, he belongs to me now," she said with a smile. "And you can't take what isn't yours."

Moros screeched even louder. The dark cloud rose high in the silo, hovering just at the entrance of the massive doors under the full moon.

"There are other pathways, other doors that are open to me. When I return, I will destroy you all," Moros hissed.

Then, with a burst of cold air, the darkness flew out into the night, leaving the silo, leaving everything in its wake to settle and still.

Selene turned and held onto Scott, kissing him until she felt a tap on her shoulder.

"I think you made your point. You two own each other," Lucas joked. "How about we get cleaned up?" he suggested, motioning to everyone standing around them.

Selene glanced down at her ruined clothes, the scratches on her arms and hands. That never could have happened had she been fighting a human. Lucas and Tara were also scratched, and Lucas had a black eye and a bloody lip.

Selene pulled Lucas into the hug with Scott and felt Tara and the rest join them. Soon, they all stood in the middle, bathed in the moonlight at the base of the silo, holding onto one another. They all laughed.

"So, does this mean you'll marry me?" Scott asked her when they had all traveled back to Michael and Xtina's place. Everyone was gathered in the living room, sipping tea, wine, or whiskey and snacking on cheese and crackers.

"Yes," she answered quickly. "But I'll want a real proposal with a ring and all," she told him, holding onto his hand.

"I can do that." Scott nodded and then kissed her.

"I can't believe that worked," Jess said with a shake of her head. "We pulled his essence out of Scott, but it was old magic that made Moros leave. I would have never thought of it. The power that the possession of love holds."

"I have the Fates to thank for that trick," Selene clarified. Then she frowned. "He'll be trying to get a corporeal form before the next fight. And, before we fight Moros again, we'll need Pandora. She will be the one to guide us to Elpis."

"Okay, we can deal with that... tomorrow," Xtina said with a sigh. "I don't know about the rest of you, but I'm exhausted."

"What happened to Mia?" Lucas asked, glancing around the room.

"Who is Mia?" Xtina asked with a frown.

"She's the djinn that I was telling you about. She helped us. The Fates seemed agitated that she was there and sent her back to where she came from. Their words, not mine," Selene told them. "I assumed she'd be at her home when I got there, but she wasn't."

"They could have sent her to the Void," Lucas suggested with a frown.

"If they did, why isn't she here now?" Scott asked. "She could leave there at any time."

"I don't know, but..." Lucas stood up suddenly. "I guess I'll go find out." He walked over and leaned down to brush a kiss on Selene's cheek and shake Scott's hand. "I'm glad the two of you are safe and happy." He turned to Tara and the rest. "It was nice meeting you. I'll be in touch." He turned back to Selene. "Don't start the next party without us, okay?"

Selene stood up and hugged Lucas again. "Be safe. Bring our genie back to us."

Lucas smiled and then, with a wave of his hand, he disappeared.

"I'm so thankful I'm not the only one who can do that now," Brea joked. "We'd better get home." She turned to Ethan as she rubbed her growing belly. "We need some rest." Ethan nodded and took Brea's hand, and they disappeared just like Lucas had.

"Where are you two staying?" Tara asked them.

Selene looked at Scott in question.

"We left all our stuff back at Mia's place. If you want, I can get us there and we can be back here in a day or two?" Selene asked Scott.

"Sounds good. Now that you have the hang of traveling like that"—he motioned to the empty spots where Lucas, Brea, and Ethan had just been—"I'm game."

Selene turned to Tara. "We'll be back in a few days. When we return, we'll use the conventional way of traveling," she added with a chuckle.

"We'll be here." Tara hugged them.

"Thanks," Scott said, looking around the room. "For stopping my father from possessing me and destroying the world."

"Anytime," Jess said as a couple people laughed.

"Ready?" Scott turned to her, and she took his hand.

"Ready." She willed them to Mia's place.

They appeared in front of the dark fireplace in Mia's empty house and embraced.

"What now?" she asked Scott after a long moment of silence.

"Now we see what is left in the fridge, then take a long hot shower, during which I plan on touching you everywhere," he said with his lips against her neck. "Then we head into the bedroom, where I will please you for hours until we finally fall asleep for a few days. After that, we head back to Atlanta and gather the rest of our stuff before heading to our new home."

"I like the sound of that. Our new home." She sighed and rested her forehead against his chest.

"I was thinking about that," Scott said, his hands brushing down her hair. "Now that I have a new position with a pretty awesome raise, since I'll technically be the bosses' brother-in-law, I think it's time we purchased a home. What do you think?"

She looked up at him and smiled. "Yeah, I can get behind that idea."

"Let's spend the next few days looking for a place to buy together." He smiled at her. "And looking for the perfect ring."

"I can get behind that idea too."

Scott frowned down at her as his hands started running over her hips. "Actually, I might amend the order of things."

"Oh?" she asked.

Scott kissed her and started pulling her down to the rug in front of the fireplace.

"Wait." She lifted her hand and shot fire from her fingertips into the waiting logs in the fireplace. "There. Now everything is perfect." She pulled Scott down onto the soft rug.

"I love you," they whispered together as they joined as one.

Lucas arrived in the place that Mia called the Void shortly after leaving Selene and the rest at the large house in Hidden Creek.

He was tired, sore, and for the first time in his life, bruised and battered. There were cuts and scratches all over his body, and he was pretty sure he had a black eye and a fat lip.

Still, they had won. At least for now.

Looking around this new place, he called out to Mia.

"She is not here," a voice said on the wind.

Lucas frowned. "Where is she?"

"Over the mountains, you must travel, over the sea, you must sail, in order to find the djinn who holds the keys," the voice chanted.

"I don't have time— " he started, but then he gasped when he realized two large iron shackles had appeared on his wrists.

"You are bound to power, and power is to thee. Until she sets you free, you must come with me." A large creature with arms and legs the length of a football field appeared before him. It was hairless, eyeless, and mouthless. Its head was almost twenty stories above him.

It was then that he realized the shackles were attached to a chain held by the large creature.

"Let me go." He tried to pull against the chains with the superior strength that he'd had all of his life. When that didn't work, he tried to fly, something he'd done for as long as he could remember, only he couldn't even jump high.

"Your power has no strength. You are as weak as a babe. I will take you to her. We shall see what we see." The being started tugging on the chain, pulling Lucas along the sandy ground.

It was then that he realized that he had no powers in Mia's world. The only one with the power to save him now was Mia. The woman he'd come here to rescue.

The Pride Series

Finding Pride

Discovering Pride

Returning Pride

Lasting Pride

Serving Pride

Red Hot Christmas

My Sweet Valentine

Return To Me

Rescue Me

A Pride Christmas

The Secret Series

Secret Seduction

Secret Pleasure

Secret Guardian

Secret Passions

Secret Identity

Secret Sauce

Secret Obsession

Secret Desire

Secret Charm

Secret Santa

The West Series

Loving Lauren

Taming Alex

Holding Haley

Missy's Moment

Breaking Travis

Roping Ryan

Wild Bride

Corey's Catch

Tessa's Turn

Saving Trace

Christmas Holly

Maggie's Match

The Grayton Series

Last Resort

Someday Beach

Rip Current

In Too Deep

Swept Away

High Tide

Sunset Dreams

Lucky Series

Unlucky In Love

Sweet Resolve

Best of Luck

A Little Luck

Christmas Wish

Silver Cove Series

Silver Lining

French Kiss

Happy Accident

Hidden Charm

A Silver Cove Christmas

Sweet Surrender

Second Chances

Entangled Series – Paranormal Romance

The Awakening

The Beckoning

The Ascension

The Presence

The Calling

The Chosen

The Beyond

Haven, Montana Series

Closer to You

Never Let Go

Holding On

Coming Home

The Hard Way

Pride Oregon Series

A Dash of Love

My Kind of Love

Season of Love

Tis the Season

Dare to Love

Where I Belong

Because of Love

A Thing Called Love

First Comes Love

Someone to Love

Fools in Love

FindingLove

Wildflowers Series

Summer Nights

Summer Heat

Summer Secrets

Summer Fling

Summer's End

Summer Wish

Summer Breeze

Summer Ride

Distracted Series

Wake Me

Tame Me

Save Me

Dare Me

Stand Alone Books

Twisted Rock

Hope Harbor

Raven Falls

Angel Bluff

Day Break

For a complete list of books:

http://JillSanders.com

ABOUT THE AUTHOR

Jill Sanders is a New York Times, USA Today, and international bestselling author of Sweet Contemporary Romance, Romantic Suspense, Western Romance, and Paranormal Romance novels. With over 85 books in eleven series, translations into several different languages, and audiobooks there's plenty to choose from. Look for Jill's bestselling stories wherever romance books are sold or visit her at jillsanders.com

Jill comes from a large family with six siblings, including an identical twin. She was raised in the Pacific Northwest and later relocated to Colorado for college and a successful IT career before discovering her talent for writing sweet and sexy page-turners. After Colorado, she decided to move south, living in Texas and now making her home along the Emerald Coast of Florida. You will find that the settings of several of her series are inspired by her time spent living in these areas. She has two sons and off-set the testosterone in her house by adopting three furry little ladies that provide her company while she's locked in her writing cave. She enjoys heading to the beach, hiking, swimming, wine-tasting, and pickleball with her husband, and of course writing. If you have read any of her books, you may also notice that there is a love of food, especially sweets! She has been blamed for a few added pounds by her assistant, editor, and fans... donuts or pie anyone?

facebook.com/JillSandersBooks

twitter.com/JillMSanders

amazon.com/Jill-Sanders/e/B009M2NFD6?tag=jillm-com-20

bookbub.com/authors/jill-sanders

instagram.com/jillsandersauthor